DEATH
THING

Andrew
Hilbert

ISBN: 978-0692666951

Published by Weekly Weird Monthly

www.weeklyweirdmonthly.com

Cover art by Jack Arambula
Author photo by Josh Verduzco

Printed in the United States of America

with each broken shoelace
out of one hundred broken shoelaces,
one man, one woman, one
thing
enters a
madhouse.

so be careful
when you
bend over.

-Charles Bukowski

GILBERT

It was the last god damn time anyone was going to break into his car. Gilbert had had enough.

"Mary, I tell you what, I'm sick and tired of these good-for-nothin' hooligans smashing my hard earned windows and stealing my shit!" Gilbert, retired and de-liberalizing with age, grabbed a beer from the fridge in the garage. "You want one?"

"No, darling. I don't drink before noon," she said.

"You would if your car was broken into twice a week!" Gilbert chuckled in a way only the truly pissed off could.

Mary was buttering toast for him when he got back into the kitchen.

"I don't know how I got so lucky," Gilbert said and sat down.

"Dear, maybe you shouldn't leave your things in plain view. Maybe the kids only break in because they see something special."

"Homeless thugs! My backseat has smelled like enchilada shit for weeks. I can't afford to pay for another window until next month. It's going to be a bum motel!"

"Cockroaches..." Mary shook her head and passed Gilbert a plate of toast.

Gilbert had an idea. Bum motel and cockroaches – those words gave him a moment of insight he hadn't had for years.

"What if... who cares right?"

"What?" Mary asked.

"Who cares... what if, right?"

"What?"

"Who cares about bums?"

"I don't know."

"Exactly," Gilbert stood up. "We have roach motels. They go in, they never come out. My car will be a death thing – a bum motel!" Gilbert smiled and his eyes penetrated the walls in front of him, his finger was pointed to the heavens and his chair became his footstool – conqueror.

"Is that even legal?"

"It doesn't matter. Smashing windows ain't legal!"

"But does the crime warrant death?" Mary put a piece of toast in her mouth. The butter dripped down her chin.

"You read the Bible. You're always telling me I should be more Christ-like. It says in there: women, don't challenge your husbands and the wages of sin is death!"

"I'm not so sure it's exactly like that," Mary said with a mouthful.

"Is that a challenge?"

Mary shut up.

Gilbert popped the cap on his beer and sipped, satisfied with his Bible quoting and plans. Mary put more toast in the toaster.

***

After a few beers, Gilbert sat on the couch in his garage making a budget for his bum motel, his death thing. It was summer, he was sweating but comfortable as ever. It was going to cost more than repairing the broken window to make this death thing but that was okay with Gilbert. A new window didn't pay for revenge.

"It's going to save money in the long run," he told Mary when she popped her head into the garage to see if he needed anything from the store. "And think of all the thieves we'll be taking off the streets."

"Do you need anything?"

Gilbert got up with a list.

"Nails, three two by fours, chicken wire, barbed wire, tarp, and plastic wrap are by far the most important immediately, but if you see it, please pick up a propane tank and some WD-40."

Mary nodded and jangled her keys next to her thigh – waiting for the inevitable next honey-do.

"Do we have any lighters?" Gilbert asked.

"Like for cigarettes?" Mary asked.

"Yes, yes, yes, of course! Jesus Christ!" Gilbert threw his hands in the air and shook his head.

"No," Mary said dead-faced. Gilbert rolled his eyes.

"Add that to the list. Maybe get more than one. I might just outfit your car with a bum motel, too."

"I don't think so."

"Just get more than one damn lighter, please."

Mary nodded as she left. Gilbert followed her, whistling.

***

Though they weren't the type of retirees that parked their cars in the garage, the next day Gilbert had his in the garage. The car radio was blaring Sinatra from decades before in defiance of the hoodlums he was preparing to teach a lesson to.

"I think I've got it," Gilbert told himself and went to the fridge for another beer.

"Keep drinking like that and you'll impale yourself," Mary said under her breath.

"Quiet!"

Gilbert popped the can and walked to the passenger side window.

"Sure, they'll smash my windows but once they reach over to unlock and open a door, the bastards'll be setting off a chain of events that they'd regret if they had the head to regret it."

Gilbert laughed.

"Just don't you dare open any of my passenger side doors. Not tonight, not tomorrow, not until I catch us our first bum."

Mary nodded and went back inside the house. She said, "I'm making tuna sandwiches if you want any."

"Fuck tuna," Gilbert said under his breath, nodded, then said, "I'll be in in a second."

***

The death thing was a simple contraption. It relied on bait. Gilbert would put his iPod or a hundred dollar bill on the front side passenger seat; this would entice the criminal to break the window, reach through where the window used to be, unlock the door from the side and pull it open. A trip wire would tug a two by four hanging on the ceiling with nothing but rusty nails hammered into it right into the criminal's head, or neck, or back and leave them there to die. Each door had this contraption fitted onto it except for the driver's side.

"It's too dangerous having a nailed up two by four hanging 'round my head when I'm driving," Gilbert once explained to his wife.

A propane tank, hidden under the front passenger seat, would constantly be flowing gas through a tube pointed at the criminal's head. Through the magic of the trip wire, pressure would be applied to the sparker and set off a blaze that only Jesus himself could save anyone from. The criminal would be impaled and burned.

Gilbert's system didn't rely solely on one method of death. Just in case the criminal broke the window and tried to climb in, nails were super glued next to the window inside of the car in hopes that the criminal wouldn't see them and get impaled.

"It's a stroke of genius," Gilbert would tell his neighbors. "My fuckin' masterpiece. I really should patent it."

***

Gilbert sat at the table chewing on his tuna sandwich and drinking another beer.

"You didn't put any pickles in the tuna," he said.

"I wanted to try something new," Mary said.

"New? New? You don't try something new by taking away ingredients. You try something new by adding them."

"You're drunk."

"Get me another beer and get me another sandwich! I have to eat more if there are no fucking pickles!"

"Get it yourself."

Gilbert, swallowing the last bit of his sandwich, stood up and went to the counter. He got two slices of wheat bread and slathered them up with mayo and mustard.

"Wheat bread..." he grumbled. "What kinda bullshit is this? You're watching too much Dr. Oz."

Mary sat in silence.

"Tasteless tuna sandwiches, not even worth my time," Gilbert said as he sat back down at the table. "You have an iPod or some hundred dollar bills or something?"

Mary slammed her tuna sandwich on her plate and groaned. "What for?"

"Don't get snippy. It's for my bum motel. My death thing! I need bait! Rats don't get pulled into rat traps for air, dummy!"

"This whole project has made you a real asshole."

"Do you have an iPod or something? Hell, maybe the grandkids left something here last weekend."

"You're not risking their toys for your sadistic games."

"Like Hell I'm not. Their toys will be safe. It's just bait."

"Ugghhh." Mary rolled her eyes and left the table. She dug through her purse for a few seconds, throwing things out in a theatrical display of annoyance.

"I can never find anything I want in my purse," she said.

"Get a smaller purse," Gilbert said in between bites of his pickle-less tuna sandwich. "Don't we have any chips or anything? You expect me to be satisfied with this when there are no pickles?"

"We don't have any chips!" Mary yelled and threw her purse at Gilbert. "Just use my purse as bait and, I swear, if my purse gets stolen you're going to get me a new one. One that's worth more than the amount of money it'll ever hold!"

"So, what? A five dollar purse?"

Mary stomped her foot on the carpet and stood, staring at Gilbert for an apology. The apology never came.

"Thanks for the purse," Gilbert said and got up for the garage.

"Going out there again?!"

"Of course. Gotta set the bait. Roaches don't come where there's no water."

"I'm going shopping!"

"Don't forget your purse!" Gilbert stepped into the garage. "Heh, heh," he chuckled to himself and threw the purse into the passenger seat.

***

"Gil! Wake up!" Mary shook Gilbert at the shoulder.

He yawned when he awoke, hung over and cotton mouthed.

"Jesus, what?!"

"You hear that?!"

There was screaming from their front yard. Screaming and moaning. Gilbert smiled.

"Go see what it is," Mary said.

"No, no, no…" Gilbert closed his eyes, "That sound means there's no need to check."

The screaming stopped. It was just moaning now. It slowed in its persistence and lowered in its volume.

"Sounds like he's giving up," Gilbert said. He rolled over and kissed Mary's forehead. "Sweet dreams, my love."

"I can't sleep. I'm going to watch some TV."

"Can you watch it in the other room? I was having a good dream. I have a feeling it's going to get better."

Without response, Mary got up and left the room.

On her way out, Gilbert asked, "Hon? Could you get me a glass of water and some ibuprofen? I'm parched."

"You shouldn't drink so damn much."

Gilbert couldn't be bothered with a lecture so much as a sentence. He rolled over in bed, closed his eyes, and, with the last weakening moan of the stranger outside, he smiled and fell asleep.

***

"Hey, Gil!" Larry, the next door neighbor, yelled to Gilbert from across the lawn.

"It's Gilbert, Larry. Only my wife can call me Gil."

"You've got something nasty hanging out of your car," Larry said.

Gilbert stepped out of his garage and looked at the car.

"I've been waiting to see this all night."

The body of a twenty-something man, bearded and with a trucker hat, hung limp outside his passenger side window. He was bloody as Hell and as dead as those who go there.

"My masterpiece," Gilbert said to himself. He turned to Larry. "This is my work of art!"

"It'll start smelling if you don't clean it up. You'll bring the property value down around here!" Larry was watering his lawn and smoking a cigarette.

"There's no value in the property 'round here anyway. You know that."

"Police know about this?"

"Who gives a shit? Just breathe it in, Larry. Breathe it in and love it. I'm cleaning up the streets of our fair city."

Larry turned around to water another patch of dead grass.

"This is La Palma. I think the cops'll want to know."

"What are they going to do? Just what are the cops going to do?" Gilbert poked at the legs of the body. They were stiff as, well, dead folks' legs. "With budget cuts and what-not, the police don't have time to protect us. They spent all their money on M-16s that they don't need. And they had to fire three officers just to be able to afford them new bullet-proof vests. It doesn't make any sense."

"Yeah," Larry said and turned back around towards Gilbert. "Kids get shorter school days, too, I hear. You know it's some bullshit when you go to 7-11 at noon and see a bunch of high schoolers drinking Gatorade and cussing in the parking lot. Those that do graduate, hell! Their diplomas don't mean shit."

"Probably the reason this asshole is hanging out of my car," Gilbert said as he grabbed the waist of the corpse and lifted it but he'd forgotten about the two by four that slammed against the poor guy's head, nailing him in place.

"Shit," Gilbert said to himself and tried as hard as he could to pry the nails out of his head. They were in there pretty good. "You gotta hammer?"

"What?" Larry turned around. He must have done ten circles in the same place the whole time he'd been out there.

"You gotta hammer handy? I've got one but I got so damn drunk yesterday, I can't remember where I put it. My death trap worked a little better than I expected."

"You set that thing up?" Larry dropped his hose and walked across his lawn and through Larry's. He stood behind Larry with his arms at his hips.

"I call this death thing the bum motel. Stopping crime as it happens. It works, too."

Larry nodded.

"I've been broken into a few times, too. Think you could set one up for me?"

"Yeah, if you help me get these nails out of this guy's fucking head."

"I don't like blood, Gil."

"It's Gilbert to you, pal."

Gilbert dropped the two by four he was trying his best to relieve from the dead man's head and got himself out of the window.

"I don't like blood, either. I also don't like fuckers trying to steal my wife's purse out of my goddamn driveway. This teaches everyone a lesson. This is a lesson this guy will never forget – it's practically stapled to his fucking head!"

"Maybe you could just park your cars in your garage," Larry said.

"That's not the point. I should be able to park my car any·damn·where any damn time I please. My wife should be able to absent-mindedly leave her purse in my car without worry about some damn hoodlum, who doesn't work hard enough to afford his own damn purse, taking it! Now, do you have a hammer or don't you?"

"Wife's using it. She's rehanging all of our family portraits."

"If you want my bum motel in your car, you'd either better get it or you'd better help me pry this fucking two by four from this fucking head and help me get this body to my shed."

Gilbert walked back into the garage and opened the door.

"Mary! Make us some fucking lemonade!"

He walked back toward Larry on his driveway.

"You grab his head and push it down. I'll pull at the two by four and, with our strength combined, we should be able to get this shit done. What do you say?"

Larry put out his cigarette on the driveway.

"I hope you're planning on washing the ash off when we're done," Gilbert said.

"Sure thing. Let me just change into a better shirt. I don't want blood all over this one. It's a nice one. Wife got it for me for our thirty year anniversary."

Gilbert's eyes were blazing into Larry's.

"Just take the fucking shirt off and help me out, you idiot."

Larry nodded and took his shirt off. He threw it on the lawn.

"Alright," Gilbert said. "Grab his head and push."

Larry reached into the car and grabbed the head at each ear. He pushed hard but with no luck. Those nails were lodged into the dead man's skull real good. Gilbert reached in around him and began tugging at the two by four as Larry pushed. Gilbert put one foot onto the car door to give him some more leverage when he pulled and bam! They both, well, all three of them, fell to the driveway. The dead man's head was bleeding all over them.

"Good thing you took off your shirt," Gilbert said and picked himself off the ground.

"This is pretty gross, Gil."

"No one said justice was easy. Get up. Help me carry him to the shed."

Larry stayed on his ass for a few minutes looking at the dead guy and shaking his head.

"I dunno, Gil. I should've had some more rum this morning. This is a little surreal."

"You have rum? You have rum?! Bring it over, you sack of shit!"

Larry got up and tried the best he could to wipe the blood off his chest. He was sweating too much so it just smeared in swirls and coagulated with his chest hair. He nodded and went back to his house.

Gilbert stood with his arms crossed toward the street. It was too early for any of the fine citizens of La Palma to be up. And if they were up, it was too early for them to care about some dead criminal on a mostly enjoyable neighbor's driveway. There definitely weren't any cops driving by. As cliché as it sounds, they really did set up their speed traps around Yum-Yum Donuts. It used to be four corners; Orangethorpe West, Walker South, Orangethorpe East, Walker North, but a dwindling economy meant for more unemployed policemen. One motorcycle cop stood on the corner of Orangethorpe and Walker just outside the Yum-Yum and pointed a radar at any red car. All of his now unemployed buddies hung out at Cliff's Hideaway, the bar in the same parking lot as Yum-Yum. When his shift relief came, he'd get a coffee at Yum-

Yum and whiskey at Cliff's. The relief always smelled like Cliff's.

"The fucking propane trap didn't go off."

Gilbert kicked the dead body on his driveway as if that was its fault.

"The fucking propane trap didn't go off!"

He kicked it again and opened the passenger side door. His hands fumbled for the propane tank and, as soon as he touched it, it went off. Fire consumed Gilbert's face and he jumped out of the car screaming and hopping around.

Larry came running, a jug of rum in his hand. He uncapped the bottle and splashed some in Gilbert's face. That only accelerated the burn.

"The hose! The hose! The fucking hose! Turn on the fucking hose!" Gilbert screamed. He slapped his face over and over again in a futile effort to put out the flames. Larry scrambled for the garden hose and turned it on full blast.

Gilbert stopped screaming. He stopped dancing around and stopped slapping his face. Chunks of flesh hung from his chin and jaw bone. His eyebrows were boiled clean off. Gilbert sat cross legged on the driveway. He could've cried had his tear ducts not been turned to scabs.

"Woah, Gil," Larry said as he turned off the hose. "You look like a monster."

Gilbert laughed a little.

"This is what crime does, Larry. You can kill a thief but they'll always come back to fuck you in the ass. Help me drag this motherfucker to the shed and take me to a hospital."

Gilbert got up and kicked the dead body. Larry grabbed the body's legs, Gilbert grabbed the arms, and they lifted.

***

"Please. Please don't fucking kiss me," Gilbert said through the bandages wrapped all over his head. Mary, who had leaned in to kiss him while he sucked a chocolate shake through a straw, turned away from him. "It hurts."

"You need to rest," she said as she got up from the bed.

Gilbert didn't answer. He kept slurping his milkshake.

"Larry dropped a bottle of rum off for you. Rum's good with chocolate," Mary said.

"Pour some in my cup, then. I'll need as much as I can to build the bum motel in his car."

Mary grunted her annoyed disagreement but poured rum into his cup anyways. She left the room without saying anything. Gilbert sat up in bed and used his straw to mix the rum into the shake. He took a sip. His lips were little more than scabs but the cold shake from the straw soothed the itching.

"Fucking bullshit," Gilbert muttered to himself and got out of bed. "Goddamn fucking bullshit."

His steps were slow – his head felt like a bowling ball filled with acid, his mind felt like golf balls banging against each other and cussing each other out at each contact. His thoughts were merely cuss words, now.

The bandages were bloody. The doctor said he'd need to put on fresh bandages every twelve hours to ensure they didn't graft with his skin. The doctor told him to stay out of the sun. As he passed Mary in the kitchen he grumbled, "Going outside to fix up Larry's fucking car with a simplified bullshit fuck exterminator."

"It's 90 degrees out there, Gil! The doctor said you need rest."

"Give me my sunglasses, then," he said. Gilbert was never good at heeding the doctor's orders.

Mary brought out his sunglasses and put them on the kitchen table without looking at Gilbert. His bandages were black with blood.

Gilbert grabbed her arm as she turned away from him.

"Look at me!"

She didn't.

"This is the face of bravery. This is the face of a man standing up to bullshit!"

Still she didn't look at him. Gilbert let go of her arm and put the sunglasses over his eyes.

"I'll need a hat," he said.

Mary brought out his *Old Guys Rule* ball cap and Gilbert put it on.

"You know I fucking hate this cap," he said, "just like you know I like pickles in my tuna sandwich, just like you know I like being looked in the eyes when I speak."

Gilbert shook his head and left for the front door. Mary started chopping pickles.

***

"My grandkids climb in and out of those windows, Gil," Larry said. He shook the ice in his glass. The rum was all gone. "I'm going inside to fix another. Want another?"

Gilbert, from inside the car's passenger seat as he hung the two by four on the ceiling panels, poked his head out and rolled his eyes. "Jesus Christ! Yes! I'm like the fucking elephant man out here!"

Yelling or talking too much caused his wounds to separate and bleed and Gilbert could feel the blood trickle down his face like sweat.

"Calm down there. Simmer, simmer," Larry said. "I'll make yours extra strong. You're bleeding through your bandages, by the way."

"It'll be a victory drink, neighbor. I'm all done here."

"I'll bring some cigars then, too," Larry said and walked into his garage.

Gilbert climbed over the center console and got out of the car on the driver's side. It was too damn dangerous to try to open the passenger door at this point. Larry only wanted one window outfitted with the trap. Any more would be too dangerous for casual driving.

Larry came back with two fuchsia and blue colored lawn chairs, two cigars, and a bottle of rum. He put the chairs on his lawn and motioned for Gilbert to sit down. Gilbert sat down and held out his glass for a healthy pour of rum. They both lit up their cigars and laughed as the cars passed them by.

"We'll clean up this town, just the two of us," Gilbert said. He took a deep draw of the cigar. "God damn," he said. "Fucking hurts to smoke."

"Drink some rum," Larry said. "Helps with a whole smattering of ailments."

Gilbert drank.

"Mmmm... mmm, sure does."

***

That night Gilbert heard moaning and yelling coming from outside. Mary tossed in her bed and kicked her blankets off and shook Gilbert awake.

"Again!? Again with this noise!?"

"Close your eyes – that's the quickest way to go to sleep," Gilbert said.

"God damn it, Gil."

Mary got up and turned on the lights in the bedroom.

"I can't sleep with this racket. Eyes closed or open."

She put on her robe and went to the front door. Gilbert didn't want to follow but he knew he had to. Mary was begging for some kind of attention and it wasn't even two hours ago that she wrapped his head in brand new bandages. He had to show some kind of solidarity.

His head pounded with each step down the hall as he followed Mary's flowing robe to the front.

"You're going out with only that on?"

"I don't have time to be decent!"

"There's hoodlums out there! There's murderers out there! There's rapists out there! You know who isn't out there? Fucking cops. They're all at Yum-Yum Donuts drinking coffee and whiskey! The only thing protecting this goddamn town is me. Now, you get back in here. Don't you dare open that damn door!"

Mary unchained the latch on the front door and turned around to face Gilbert. She wasn't wearing anything but her night slip, one breast hung out of the armpit slit.

"I don't care!"

"At least put on a shirt, dammit!"

"I don't care!"

"At least tie up your damn robe!"

"I don't care!"

She turned away from Gilbert, undid the lock chain, unbolted the bolt, unlocked the lock, and opened the door.

Gilbert's car was clean and empty. No roaches were staying in that motel. But outside of Larry's passenger door drooped a body, still wriggling but stuck, caught with nowhere to go.

Mary froze and stared at the scene.

"Get back in the god damn house."

Gilbert grabbed her arm and pulled her towards him.

"Look away," he said.

Tears fell from Mary's eyes. No words escaped her thoughts.

She slapped Gilbert. He felt his wounds reopen and his skin loosen their grip on his face. He was bleeding through his bandages... again. But Gilbert said nothing and Mary said nothing. She walked back into the house and left the door open for him. Gilbert walked to Larry's car.

"You scumbag," he said to the struggling would-be thief. "I'm not going to save you or put you out of your misery. I'm going to let you slap around like a fucking fish and think about how worthy breaking into to people's cars actually is."

The two by four was securely fastened to the thief's head. He bled and gasped for air and tried to turn around to face his accuser but couldn't. He was face down on the ass of the seat, nails ensuring he couldn't move.

Gilbert spit on the dying man's head and walked back into his house. He didn't go to the bedroom; Mary would have just as soon kicked him out. He sat on his reclining chair, closed his eyes, and fell asleep with a smile scarred onto his face.

***

It wasn't until noon that Gilbert got up the next day. Mary was in the kitchen with Larry's wife, Bernadette, drinking coffee.

"He's beside himself right now," Bernadette said as she stirred the milk into her coffee.

"I can't even talk about Gilbert right now. His scheming has changed him."

"Ugh," Bernadette said. "Let's not even talk about the boys right now. I'm trying to pass the Bechdel test."

Gilbert got up from the recliner and went to the kitchen.

"What's for lunch?"

Mary looked up to him and shook her head. She got up and gave him a plate. A tuna sandwich.

"Pickles?" Gilbert asked.

"Yes, honey," she said, "and plenty of mustard."

Gilbert took a bite.

"What'd you do to Larry?" Bernadette was stirring her coffee unnecessarily. The spoon clinked against her mug.

"To Larry?" Gilbert asked.

"Go outside and talk to him," Bernadette stopped stirring and took a sip of her coffee.

"How do I look?" he asked Mary. His bandages were black with dried blood. Gilbert could feel his scabs crack as he chewed.

"You look fine. Go out and talk to Larry. I'll change your bandages later. I need some time to myself."

Gilbert went to the restroom and pissed. He looked in the mirror at his bandages and ran his fingers over them. They were hard as plaster with dried blood. He smiled.

"The wounds of war," he said to himself. "There's no victory without it." He put on his sunglasses and his cap and left.

When he got outside, Larry was sitting on a lawn chair on his driveway taking deep swigs of his bottle of rum and sobbing. He didn't turn to face Gilbert even though his shadow had overtaken him.

"He fucking shit his pants, Gil," Larry said. "He fucking shit all over himself."

"Smells like it," Gilbert said and reached for Larry's bottle of rum. Larry denied it to him and held it close to his chest.

"It sure fucking does smell like it." Larry took another swig from the bottle. "I heard him all night moaning and crying. I can't do this."

"Oh, shut up. You had no problem when it was a dead guy on my driveway. Now that the war has breached your lawn, you're tucking your penis between your legs and crying."

"It's just that it smells so bad. I don't know that my iPad is really worth this kind of protecting..." Larry stared at the puddle of shit and blood on the concrete.

"That was a good piece of bait, the iPad," Gilbert tried to console him.

"It's not worth it."

"Shut up! If it wasn't your iPad it would've been somebody else's. Now it's nobody's and never will be at the hands of this fucking useless piece of crap. Man up. Let's get this body out of here."

Larry shook his glass and looked into it. His face was blank but he stared through the rum and to the bottom where the ice was melting. There was no way out of it – the glass of rum didn't tell him that but he stared hoping he'd drink enough to die – so he got up and grabbed the dead man by the legs and pulled at them.

"It smells so bad," he said.

He tugged harder. The body stayed in place. It was stuck on the nails hammered through the power window slats.

Gilbert, impatient, grabbed at the dead man's waist and tugged too. It was as if the sound of his shirt and flesh ripping through the nails as the body slumped over onto the driveway had no effect on Gilbert. But Larry, Larry burst into tears.

"God damn it," Gilbert said. "I'll drag this son of a bitch to my shed and you just go inside, drink some more, and get some rest."

Larry grabbed his bottle of rum and glass of melted ice and walked into his house through the garage. Gilbert dragged the body across Larry's driveway and through his front lawn. A trail of blood followed him. Gilbert could feel beads of his own blood soaking through his bandages and falling onto the dead body.

Mary and Bernadette stared through the front window, their eyes were wide and looked like empty sockets over their gaping mouths. Gilbert turned to them.

"Go back in the fucking kitchen!" he yelled. "I'm hungry!"

***

"Bernadette called me when she got home tonight in tears," Mary said to Gilbert as he took off his socks and pants and got ready for bed.

"Yeah, well," he said, "women are more emotional than men."

Mary cleared her throat.

"I could hear Larry wailing in the background, Gil."

"Never said Larry was a man, dear." Gilbert went to the restroom and sat on the toilet. He could hear Mary continue with her story that he didn't want to hear but he answered with *yeah*s and *uh-huh*s anyways.

Her voice was muffled through the door but Gilbert could hear her going on and on. He could pick out only the words he expected her to say: Larry, Bernadette, bandages, shed, etc.

"Yeah, uh-huh," Gilbert nodded in the bathroom. "Listen, darling, I'm trying to use the restroom. I can't concentrate on our neighbors' marital struggles."

He heard the bed creak and footsteps come towards the bathroom door.

"You've become such a jerk!"

That was the first full sentence he'd heard in two minutes.

"Loud and clear, honey," Gilbert said and flushed.

The sound of the toilet flushing and refilling itself with fresh water lingered, as Gilbert tried to stay in the restroom for as long as possible to avoid Mary's anger but the sound of a shotgun blast from outside deafened him. The world went white as he launched into survival mode.

Mary wailed.

"Mary!?" he yelled, forgetting to buckle or even zip his pants up. He burst out of the bathroom with his pants sagging down his waist toward his knees. He hitched them up again and waddled out to her. She was on the floor screaming.

"Mary!" he knelt beside her and cradled her in his arms. She wasn't bleeding. "What happened?"

"It...it came from outside!" she yelled.

Gilbert stood up, his pants at his ankles, and walked out the front door.

Bernadette was outside with the shotgun at her hip, pointed to Gilbert.

"Back away, Gil," she said. "Back the fuck away."

Gilbert had his hands up but he inched closer to her. He couldn't go more than an inch at a time, his pants at his ankles significantly hindered his approach but he barely noticed it.

"I hate being called Gil," he said. He could feel his bandages sticking to his face, wet with blood and sweat.

"Oh, fuck you," she said and raised the shotgun. "You turned Larry into some groveling idiot. You're all too afraid to face this fucking problem head on. Buy a gun, Gil. Buy a fucking gun and shoot these thugs with some conviction, not some rat trap that kills impersonally and from a distance."

Gilbert didn't notice it at first but a body lay bleeding in between Gilbert's and Larry's yard. He was moaning.

"This fucking rat was looking into your windows. I was putting groceries away when I saw him so I went inside, took my shotgun, and blew his ass away as soon as he realized he was going to die."

The man on the ground turned his head toward Gilbert and moaned – begged through indecipherable gargles of blood for Gilbert's help.

"He ain't dead yet," Gilbert said.

"Larry's too much of a pussy to finish him off. He's inside crying again. Calls himself a man."

"Half the neighborhood is peering through their windows right now because of the sound of your gun. That's the point of my death thing — avoiding a commotion, avoiding breaking honest people's sleep. It's not about being a man, it's about taking out the trash without breaking the neighborhood's routine."

Gilbert shuffled toward the dying man.

"Are you going to kill this bastard or are you going to keep complaining about your husband?"

Bernadette walked to the body with the shotgun and, without looking, shot again. Blood spattered all over both of them.

"Now he's in a million little pieces. Who's going to clean him up?" Gilbert asked.

That snapped Bernadette out of her death-trance. Her chin quivered and tears welled in her eyes.

"I don't know!" she yelled between sobs and fell to her knees.

Gilbert, finally noticing that his pants were at his ankles, hitched them up again and said, "Go get Larry. We'll take care of it."

***

Larry came outside sometime after Gilbert started scooping pieces of bone and flesh with a shovel from the grass into a trash bag. Larry's eyes were swollen.

"At least most his body's still intact," Gilbert said. "It wouldn't be a walk in the park otherwise."

Larry nodded.

"How's Bernadette?" Gilbert asked.

Larry didn't answer.

Gilbert tied up the trash bag he was done filling and handed it to Larry.

"We're going to put this in somebody's trunk," he said. "The shed's running out of space and soon I'll have to figure out how to get rid of them, too."

"Somebody's trunk?" Larry asked. "Isn't that a little unfair?"

"No one asked your wife to go lighting the neighborhood on fire with a shotgun," Gilbert answered. "We'll put it into some drug dealer's or otherwise contemptible figure in the community's trunk."

"How would you decide who's suspicious enough for this?"

"The fact that they have a body in the trunk makes them suspicious enough."

Larry nodded. Gilbert stood up.

"C'mon," he said. "It'll be easy."

Gilbert passed Larry the bag of face and head parts and Gilbert dragged the body by the ankles. They passed by many homes before Gilbert stopped.

"The guy who lives here," Gilbert said, "I think he's a drug dealer. I see streams of people come in and out of there, night after night."

Larry nodded without looking in Gilbert's direction. His eyes stayed on the trash bag.

"He's our mark," Gilbert said and dropped the body's ankles to the sidewalk. He walked up to the trunk and tried pushing in the keyhole to open it. That would have worked on an unlocked Mercedes but not on a Honda Civic, locked or unlocked.

Breaking his silence, Larry said, "Try the front doors. If he left it unlocked, you'll be able to pop the trunk. No problem."

"He speaks!" Gilbert looked up to the cloudless night in praise. Larry didn't acknowledge it. He kept his head down. Gilbert opened the driver's side door.

"Well, it's unlocked!" Gilbert leaned inside and looked for a lever or a button that would pop the trunk. "What am I looking for?"

Larry dropped the trash bag and reached into the driver's left side on the floor and pulled a lever, clearly labeled with a trunk symbol. The trunk popped. Larry went back to the bag and grabbed it and still said nothing.

"Fucking creep," Gilbert muttered to himself as he closed the front door shut. He grabbed the ankles of the body. "Grab his arms, help me lift him in."

Larry did as he was told.

Once the body was stuffed in the trunk, Gilbert grabbed the trash bag, tied it into a knot, and shoved it in. Gilbert slammed the trunk, Larry screamed, and the trunk didn't close.

Larry was holding his right hand and screaming. It was bloody and mangled.

"Shut up before anyone hears you, you fucking idiot!"

Larry closed his eyes, cradled his hand close to his chest, and did his best not to scream. He whimpered.

"Keep it down," Gilbert said without looking at him and slammed the trunk down again. It didn't close.

"What in the hell?"

Gilbert looked around for anything that could be obstructing the trunk from closing. He climbed into the trunk and tamped the body down with his foot like he did the kitchen trash can when he was too lazy to tie it up and throw it out. Larry's whimpering provided the melody to the body tamping percussion. All of these sounds annoyed Gilbert. He climbed back out of the trunk and tried shutting it again.

It didn't shut.

"God damn it!" Gilbert kicked the bumper. He turned to Larry. "Any ideas?"

Larry shook his head.

"I need a drink," he said.

"Then go get one! Fuck!" Gilbert tried slamming the trunk again. It didn't close. Out of sheer rage, he slammed about a thousand times and never once thought the next time that it was going to do the trick. He was right. It never did.

Larry came back with a bottle of rum tucked under his armpit. He was still cradling his bad hand in his good one. He handed the bottle to Gilbert.

"Can you uncap it for me?" he asked.

"You've said five fucking words tonight and your next five are for a fucking favor?"

Larry looked to the sky and tried counting how many words were in his last sentence.

"Yes! Yes! Yes!" Gilbert said as he uncapped the bottle of rum. "Of course I'll uncap it for the sweet prince with the mangled hand!" He took a nip at it and handed it back to Larry. He could feel the scabs on his face breathing and sweating underneath his bandages. "My fucking face gets burned off and nobody does any favors for me," he said as he stood back up. "This whole town is made of ingrates and invalids. The ingrates are the ones breaking into cars and the invalids are too busy shitting their pants to stop them."

As he ranted, Larry's eyes went from dumb and sad to focused and intent. He was staring right at the car's bumper as Gilbert went on and on about the state of La Palma and how he should probably just walk away from being its Batman.

"This guy got rear-ended," Larry said. He chugged at his rum. "This guy definitely got rear-ended."

"And what the hell is that supposed to mean to me?!" Gilbert was livid. He flailed his arms and his bandages started to come undone from around his face. He was dripping blood.

"Gil, calm down. Jesus Christ." Larry took another glug of rum. "Years ago I was hit from behind. Little tiny fender bender but bend my fender, it did. The trunk gets all misaligned sometimes and the locking mechanism doesn't quite fit. You can probably finagle it a bit to get it going, but slamming it over and over again ain't going to work. Here," Larry passed the bottle to Gilbert, "take a nip of this and take a breather. Calm down. That's the only way it's going to work."

Gilbert put the bottle to his lips but Larry stopped him before he could sip.

"Wipe your face off, you're going to get blood all over the bottle."

Gilbert felt his bandages wet with blood and took his shirt to them. As soon as he wiped off his lips he put the bottle to them again and took a hearty sip.

"Now, breathe in and forget about whatever you're pissed off about," Larry said, "and take another sip to help with the forgetting."

Gilbert took another sip.

"I don't know why I'm taking orders from you. Just a minute ago you were crying like a pussy and now you're a Buddhist fucking monk."

"I'm not giving you orders. We're in this together. Now, I'd do this myself if you hadn't slammed the trunk on my hand but just look at the trunk and see where the hook latches. You're going to have to pull that hook out as far as it goes for as long as you can as you close the door and hope it latches. Might take a couple tries. Oh, well. We've got rum."

Gilbert studied the trunk. He looked at the latching mechanism and what it was connected to. It seemed simple. All he needed to do was hold pull the latch for long enough so that it'd reach the bar as he slammed it down.

"I'm going to smash my fucking fingers," he said.

"It isn't so bad," Larry said.

He tried it but his nerves stopped him from holding it long enough. The trunk slammed and then rose up again.

"God dammit."

He tried again. And again. And again.

"Fuck."

Gilbert stared down at his shoes.

"Maybe if we use a shoelace to pull the latch..."

"Then there'd be a shoelace hanging outside the trunk when it's done," Larry said and sipped his rum. The bottle was damn near finished.

"I doubt this pot head would even notice."

Gilbert bent down to his shoe, untied it, and stripped the lace from it. He tied a knot around the latch and handed the shoe lace to Larry.

"Hold it taut as I slam the trunk. It'll work. I swear it will."

Larry stood directly in front of the latch and took enough steps backwards so that there was no slack in the shoelace.

"All right, I'm slamming on the count of three. One, two, three."

The trunk slammed shut.

"Let's fucking celebrate. You think Cliff's is still open?"

"It's only midnight," Larry said. "Let's go."

The shoelace, bloodied from Larry's mangled hand, dangled outside the trunk.

***

"I don't think I can continue with this shit, Gil," Larry said, his bad hand in his lap and his good hand warming his pint glass on the table.

They sat at the back of the bar next to the toilets and under the dartboard that nobody ever played. The TVs all over the bar were each at high volume, playing different baseball games. There were only four tables in the whole bar. Most patrons sat at the bar, ass cracks creeping above their jeans, with their heads on the bar in puddles of their own spilled beer. Gilbert recognized a few off duty cops sitting at a booth close enough to the entrance to escape if any trouble broke out.

"You're fighting a war. I'm not even affected by taking out the trash anymore. I thought you were a stronger man." Gilbert poured some more beer into each of their glasses. Their pitcher was almost empty. He motioned for the bartender to bring another. "And don't call me Gil."

"Look, goddammit. It was a good idea when I was watching you from my front yard. It was a good idea. It was. Jesus Christ," Larry said, "I can't even get the words out of my mouth."

Gilbert scratched at his bandages that hadn't been changed in too long. His face was on fire.

"As soon as the action came to my front yard, as soon as I had to come to grips with the fact that somebody died because of *me* on *my* property, I lost it. My wife can't even look at me anymore."

The waitress topped off their beers from the first pitcher and put another in front of them.

"That's why you keep fighting," Gilbert said. "You keep fighting. You don't turn around and run. You keep fighting."

"It's too dirty," Larry said. "I can't be getting rid of dead bodies all the time. I used to water my lawn so that grass would grow. Tomorrow morning, I'm going to have to wash the left over bone and brain off my yard and into the street. Just thinking about it makes me sick."

"You're discounting your own strengths. Your quick thinking closed that trunk."

"That was survival, Gil. Jesus Christ. You were slamming that trunk so hard, I'm surprised the cops weren't called."

Larry stood up and threw some money on the table.

"Don't call me Gil."

"What's it to you, anyways? Who cares what I call you?"

"Only my wife can call me Gil."

"Afraid I'm going to fuck you?" Larry said and started to walk away only to find his face in the green polo shirt of an off-duty officer.

"What's this I hear about calling the cops and wives fucking?" he asked.

Larry tried to walk past him but the cop pushed him back toward the table.

"Sit down," he said and sat down himself to join the conversation he wasn't invited to. "So, what's up? What's going on? Can I pour myself something?"

Larry and Gilbert sat there, quiet, staring at the wood grain pattern on their table.

"Waitress!" the off duty cop said, "Get us some fucking peanuts!"

"Sure thing, Bob O!"

The waitress must have been 80 years old. Her lips sagged around a dangling cigarette, her makeup flaked around her eyes. Her hair was bleached with the yellow stain of tobacco. She threw a bowl of peanuts on the table.

"These guys wanted it added to their tab." Bob pointed to Gilbert and Larry.

"Sure thing, Bob O!"

Bob grabbed a handful of peanuts and put two in his mouth.

"I like to suck all the salt off first," he said as he took one out and cracked it in his hands. He threw the nuts in his mouth like they were pills, poured himself a drink, and washed them down with beer. "So you guys want to explain what this was I heard about dead bodies, so-and-so's yard, and so on and so forth?" He chewed his peanuts and refilled his mouth with them in between words.

Larry got silent again, like he was all night, and continued to stare at the wood grain and the way that beer puddled on to it even though he was sure he hadn't spilled at all.

"Well... Bob O, is it?"

Bob nodded as he sucked on another salted peanut shell.

"What's the O stand for in Bob O anyway?"

"Stands for Officer. Bob Officer. Usually..." Bob paused to pick a red peanut skin out of his front teeth, "Usually people call people by their title and then their last name. Darla, sweet old lady she is, calls me by my first name first and then my title. She thinks it's funny," Bob chuckled, "I do, too."

Gilbert looked through Bob's eyes as he chuckled and threw peanuts down his throat.

"Funny, ha," he said. "We're talking about necessity, me and my friend Larry here are. I don't know what the La Palma Police Department does all day but every God damn time I do see them, they're either in here or writing speeding tickets. My car's been broken into four hundred god damn times!"

"Sorry to hear that. You've got to understand, tho – "

"I don't have to understand a damn thing, Bobby. All I have to understand is what's going on in and around my house and I understand it damn well. While the La Palma Police Department is drinking beer and eating peanuts, hoodlums break into my car and, God damn it, I ain't taking it anymore."

"I hear you," Bob said as he grabbed the pitcher and poured some beer into his empty mug.

"You're going to pay for that pitcher and you're going to pay for those peanuts," Gilbert said. He could feel his bandages, wet again, his scabs tearing apart from his skin as he sweated. His face was never going to heal.

"Sir," Bob said, "you really have to understand my situation here."

Gilbert stood up.

"Let's go," he said. "Pretend Officer Bobby here wants me to hear some sob story about a police officer's salary and so on and so on. I'm not hearing it anymore."

"Come on, guys," Bob said. "Sit back down, come on." He tapped the seat next to him.

Gilbert sat back down.

"You order the next pitcher," Gilbert said.

"Guys," Bob O put his hands in the air and shrugged his shoulders, "Come on. I'm a La Palma cop. My M16 has a bigger salary."

Larry stared at the wood grain patterns on the table. Without looking up, he said, "I'll buy the next fucking pitcher if we can all just get to the point."

"Guy's got a mouth, don't he?" Bob said.

"Not until just now. Jesus Christ," said Gilbert. He motioned for another pitcher and it came. They refilled their glasses.

"So what is it you fellas have been doing that the cops can't do?"

"I've built a bum motel," Gilbert said. He let the words hang in the space between them. Bob O's face betrayed his inner vacancy. The words hung there for too long. "A fucking death trap in my car. My car's been broken into so many damn times, the cops never do anything, the bad guys keep coming back. I'm sick of it."

"Death trap, eh? Kind of like a rat trap?" Bob O wasn't the finest boy in blue. "How many, eh, rats have you trapped?" Bob leaned over the basket of peanuts to hear whatever Gilbert was going to answer.

"A few."

Bob slumped back in his chair. He scratched his head as he let the confession of crime in a casual setting sink in.

"You're right," he said. "The cops can't do that. Pretty illegal."

Gilbert pounded the rest of his beer and stood up. Larry stood up, too.

"Well, cuff me, officer." Gilbert held up his hands.

Officer Bob dismissed them.

"Sit back down, Jesus H. Christ, I'm not going to arrest you. You guys know we've been up to our ears in budget cuts. You catch enough rats, pretty soon you start noticing there's no more rat shit all over your house. You kill the rats, we have less rat shit to worry about, keep the costs down, maybe some of my unemployed brothers in arms can get their jobs back." Bob poured himself another beer. "How do you guys do it anyway? What's the trick?"

Gilbert smiled. His scabbed and dried lips cracked as he did. It'd been a long time.

"A two by four with a ton of rusty nails comes crashing down on their skulls as they break into the window. Sure, they struggle a bit, shit their pants, but, eventually they give up the ghost."

"You bait 'em?" Officer Bob was leaning over the table so close to Gilbert's face that they were practically kissing.

"Of course we bait them. If we don't bait them, they break into some other poor sucker's car. Throw an iPad, a purse, hell, throw a five dollar bill on the passenger seat and the roaches come out of the sewers."

Officer Bob slumped back into his chair. He combed his mustache with his finger as he thought.

"Well, shit," he said. "You gotta figure out a less brutal way of offing these folks. Some people won't have the stomach for this kind of thing. You wouldn't want them calling me about you, would you?"

"It's the cleanest method I can afford," Gilbert said.

They sat there, quiet, for a few minutes. The waitress came to the table and pointed to Larry.

"If he ain't drinking, he ain't welcome. Besides, we're closing in five minutes. Who's paying?"

They sat there, quiet, for a few minutes.

Bob got up.

"Well, boys. I'm sure you'll figure something out. We'll stay out of your way if you stay out of the headlines."

"Goodnight, Bob O," the waitress smiled through her lipstick.

"Horseshit," Gilbert said. He threw a twenty on the table and left. Larry followed.

"This isn't enough, you son of a bitch!" the waitress yelled as they walked out the door.

"Charge Bob O next time he's in."

***

The garage was hot and the air was stale. Gilbert hammered away at something, many things, but never felt satisfied enough to get up and say he was finished. He sat on the couch in the garage and took a break with a bottle of whiskey and turned the radio up. It was Dean Martin. Gilbert hummed along and nodded his head.

The first thing every morning and the last thing every night

Gilbert smiled. Dean Martin sounded just as drunk as Gilbert was on the recording.

"Everyone's best work is done with drink," he closed his eyes and let the music overcome him.

Mary walked in.

"What is it?" Gilbert asked before she could say anything.

"The police are at the door for you," Mary said. "Gil, what's going on?"

"Agh," Gilbert stood up, "don't worry about those idiots. They can't even afford peanuts. Really."

Gilbert hitched his pants up and slapped himself a few times to wake himself up. He was used to the feeling of his scabs reopening and bleeding through his bandages by now.

"Call Larry over here. He'll want to be around for this, guaranteed," Gilbert said. He clicked the garage door opener on the wall and the garage opened. Gilbert had to squint, the light was green. He was inside for too long, working too hard, and drinking too much. He grabbed his sunglasses in his front shirt pocket and put them over his eyes.

"Well, there they are. The boys in blue!"

Bob O was there chewing on gum. Two officers flanked him. They were also chewing gum and wearing sunglasses.

"Geez, looks like you all belong to some weird sex cult," Gilbert said. "Ha!"

The boys in blue were not amused.

"We came here to help," Bob O said.

Gilbert took a swig of whiskey.

"As if I need any."

Bob O turned to his partners and smirked. They nodded their heads.

"Well, it seems to me that you're taking part in some dirty vigilantism. Normally, we'd have to do something about you. Seeing as how things are the way they is, we figure having you doing some contract work for us couldn't hurt."

"Uh-huh." Gilbert nodded and stumbled back and forth as he tried to stay straight.

"Where are the bodies?" Bob O asked between gum chews.

Gilbert, left leg in front of right leg, and then right leg in front of left leg, in a constant battle to stay standing, wobbled in circles in front of the officers.

"Come again, Bobby?" Gilbert said, the world spinning around him.

"The bodies," Bob O said, his mustache twirling in and out of existence in Gilbert's eyes, "where are you keeping them? We can clean them up. Keep things quiet."

"In the backyard. In the shed. In the shed in the backyard. In the shed in the backyard behind my house. They stink, heh-heh! They stink real good, boys! Have a fun time cleaning them up!"

Bob O smiled and patted Gilbert on the back.

"Get some rest. You need to find a cleaner method. But first, get some rest."

Gilbert stumbled backwards and fell on his ass.

"What do you think I'm working on right now?"

"A hangover," Bob O said. "Get up, go to sleep. We'll take care of the bodies."

"You take care of my body, I'll be sleeping."

Gilbert shuffled back into the garage and closed it. He didn't look behind, he'd have seen the cops laughing at him. He fell into the kitchen table, banging his head before hitting the ground. The bandages were a deep red, fresh blood mixing with the dried, hours-old stuff. He closed his eyes but the world was still spinning.

"Get me a fuckin' tuna sandwich, dammit, with some pickles, extra mustard," he said as he fought the urge to puke. "And a fuckin' beer, my dear."

His head lay in a puddle of pink vomit and he fell asleep.

***

"Heard you had a rough one yesterday, Gil," Larry crossed the lawn with a glass of rum in his hand. He had an umbrella in it. He wore silver tinted aviators, a fisherman's hat, a Hawaiian shirt, and a cigarette dangled between his lips. He was a poor man's Hunter S. Thompson.

Gilbert pointed to the bandages around his head.

"Barfing got the wife to change them for me, though. Ain't all bad."

"Hungover?"

"A little."

"Saw the cops over yesterday, Gil. What was their deal?" Larry blew smoke into the sky and watched it disappear. He covered his eyes with his hands to get a better view of the smoke's dissipation.

"Same old shit. Bob O was with 'em. Offered to clean up the bodies. I haven't even checked the shed yet. You want to come with?"

"I don't know if I can stomach it, Gil."

"Stop calling me Gil for Christ's sake. Only my wife can call me that and even then, it's irritating."

Larry took a sip of his rum and scratched his head.

"Okay. Did you tell them about the body in the trunk?" asked Larry.

"No, of course not. That body's there. It's on somebody else's property, it's their fucking problem," Gilbert stopped walking and turned to Larry. He pointed to his head. "I live up here, Larry. Right up here, and all I worry about is me now."

Larry swirled what was left of his rum in his glass. The ice was melting.

"What about me, Gil? You worry about me?"

Gilbert sighed, turned around, and kept walking.

"Jesus Christ, Larry. I only worry about you in relation to me. You should only worry about me in relation to you. And stop calling me Gil."

When they opened the shed, it was spotless. Cleaner, even, than before Gilbert had started stuffing bodies into it. Everything was in what appeared to be its proper place.

"I've been looking for this shovel for years," Gilbert said. He grabbed the shovel off a rack and pretended he was going to hit Larry over the head with it.

"Calm down, Gil! Shit!"

"Relax, I'm not going to kill you."

"Well, fuck, I don't know that. Anymore at least."

They stood in silence as they marveled at what the boys in blue had done to Gilbert's shed.

"I could sleep out here if I wanted to, you know," Gilbert said.

"Aren't you afraid it's haunted?"

"I ain't afraid of no ghost."

Gilbert walked to his lawnmower that he hadn't used in years since he hired a landscaping company to take care of his ten square foot yard. It was shiny. The layers of dust and mud had been cleaned off and its true color, fire engine red, could finally be seen.

"There was probably lots of blood all over this thing. The police had to clean it up real good," Gilbert said as he admired it. "I oughta mow the lawn," he said. "For old time's sake."

"I should get going. Bernadette will have my nuts for dinner if I stay any longer."

Gilbert wasn't listening. He put the lawn mower on its side and looked at the blades.

"They even buffed the blades," he said as he ran his finger on the sharp side. "Why would they want to do that?"

"They gotta be thorough, Gil. Real thorough like. You can't have any loose ends. They're in this shit deep now."

Gilbert touched his bandages. They were dry. He wasn't bleeding for the first time in days.

"No, no," he said. "Blades are the answer. What was that thing they used in the French Revolution?"

"Aw, fuck, I don't know." Larry was bored without a glass full of rum. "What's it to you?"

"That fucking thing that chopped heads off... what was it?"

"Le Chateau Marmot," Larry said. The ice in his glass had turned to water and he slurped it up, ready to turn around and walk back home.

Gilbert shook his head. His reflection was staring back at him on one of the blades. He smudged it out with a fingerprint.

"It was a guillotine. The god damn guillotine. That's the answer. That's cleaner! No more prying some guy's head off of a two by four. Once the head goes, it's gravy town from there. No struggle."

"Guillotine Gil, they'll call ya," Larry said.

Gilbert nodded and smiled. Nobody knew he was smiling underneath his bandages, not even his reflection could see it, but it was a genuine smile. His lips cracked as they spread across his face. His scabs loosened and he started bleeding again but like hell if it wasn't an actual smile.

***

He was possessed. Locked away in the garage, he made sure to tell Mary to stay out of his way while he was working. She was only allowed to break his concentration if she had food for him. His car was pulled into the driveway. All of the doors were open and he was tinkering with the power windows.

"Ah ha," he said to himself when he thought he was figuring something out.

He took off the driver's side door panel to get a closer look of how exactly the windows rolled up and down. The lawnmower was in the garage, too, completely dismantled, the four blade cutters on the ground.

"Guillotines chop falling, power windows roll up," he said to himself. His guillotine, it was obvious now, would have to work in reverse.

Fueled by cheap beer and shitty whiskey, Gilbert worked into the night. His radio was loud, his thoughts were louder. He had a trip system set up on all windows but the driver's side. It'd be too dangerous if someone was driving to accidentally set off the trip and cut off their own ear. The driver's side had to be controlled traditionally, by pushing the window button. This was there as assurance. Maybe someone would lean into his car in hopes of carjacking him. They'd lose their arm or their head if Gilbert was quick enough with the button.

He cut off a quarter of each window and super glued the blades to the tops of them. It was a primitive system but it'd do its job. He jerry-rigged the windows to move at twice their normal speed. Nobody would see the guillotine coming and by the time they did, they'd be staring at their own headless necks.

Gilbert's watch read two in the morning. It'd been a long day and Mary hadn't even brought him any food. He was too busy to know his hunger. He didn't care. He rolled up the garage and backed the car into the driveway. It was primetime for thugs.

He left every window rolled down. He left a wallet on the front passenger side seat, his cell phone in the back seat.

He walked backwards into the garage and admired his death thing for every moment he could as the garage rolled down.

"Mary!" he yelled. "I need a change of bandages!"

***

"Three heads," Gilbert yelled on his driveway. "Three heads and three bodies! Yee-haw!"

Larry was sitting in his lawn chair, rum in hand, staring at Gilbert.

"Guillotine Gil gets 'em again!" he said.

"Why don't you come over here and help me put them in the shed?"

Larry stopped smiling.

"Nope," he said. "Not going to do it, Guillotine. I'm done with the body cleaning business. I'd rather watch it happen than get my hands dirty."

Gilbert shook his head. He grabbed one of the bodies from the ankles and dragged him to the backyard. He dragged the next two there, too. Blood stains marked the trail. The shed was too clean to fill with dead bodies anyway.

"Now for the heads," he said to himself.

The first one sat upright in the passenger seat in a puddle of coagulated blood.

"Son of a bitch. My car's all dirty."

"Not clean enough, eh, Guillotine?" Larry toasted the air and slurped down his rum.

Gilbert didn't mind being called Guillotine so he didn't respond.

"You got any plastic bags?" he asked.

"Somewhere in my garage. I'll go take a looksee."

Two heads sat in the leg space in the backseat. Their lips were touching, their eyes wide open and expressions frozen from the moment they lost their bodies. Gilbert couldn't help but laugh.

"Fucking queers," he said to himself, picked up each one by the ears, and set them on the driveway.

"Got a bag! One of those thick Target bags!" Larry said from his lawn.

"Bring it to me!"

"Nope. No can do, Guillotine Gil. I only appreciate this kind of violence from the comfort of my lawn. I can't be a part of it anymore."

"Jesus Christ." Gilbert walked to Larry and snatched the bag out of his hand. "Got any rum for me?" he asked.

Larry handed him the bottle.

"Take a swig," he said.

Gilbert walked back to the car with the bottle in his hand. He took horse sips every step.

"I didn't say you could have the whole thing!"

"It's the wimp tax," Gilbert said and took another swig.

He put all three heads in the bag and walked it to the backyard. As he walked back to his driveway, he noticed the blood stains all over the concrete and turned on the garden hose and watered it down.

"Watering concrete, eh, Guillotine Gil?" Larry laughed. "Say, bring back that bottle!"

Gilbert finished it off and threw the bottle on Larry's lawn. When he was done watering, he went into his garage, closed it, and walked into the house.

Larry sat on his lawn chair alone.

"What happened out there?" Mary asked Gilbert as he walked in. He was covered in blood, not just his face bandages, either.

"Three dead crooks, my love. Three dead crooks rotting in our backyard. They really lost their heads."

"I don't like what you've become," Mary said and sat at the kitchen table. "We need to talk."

"We don't need to talk nothing!" Gilbert took off his shirt. "I'm taking a shower. I expect to be re-bandaged when I'm through."

"Bandage yourself, you old murderer!" Mary threw a butter knife, left over from breakfast, at Gilbert. It hit him right between the eyes.

Gilbert rushed Mary and grabbed her by the elbows. Her legs dangled as he lifted her in the air. She screamed and yelled and Gilbert stared right into her eyes as they open and shut with each exhalation of fear. He smiled, the skin around his lips cracked and bled, but it was a real smile. He set her down.

"I'm taking a shower. When I'm through, you better wrap the bandages and gauze around my face. I'm not taking no shit today."

Mary nodded, put her head in her hands, and sobbed.

Gilbert unbuckled his belt and, as he walked to the bathroom, let his pants fall off with each step. He left them in the hall for Mary to clean up after him.

***

"You son of a bitch," Mary said as she wrapped the bandages around Gilbert's face.

"That's too tight, Mary, that's too tight. You're going to flatten my nose into my face."

But she didn't listen. She kept wrapping. Layer after layer, she wrapped it tight over his mouth so it'd be a struggle for him to talk. She made sure his ears were pasted to the sides of his face and that the bandages applied as much pressure to his eyeballs as her own fingers would if she had her way.

It crossed her mind that she could strangle him.

There he was, naked and still damp from the shower, sitting in the middle of the kitchen on a stool. His back was to her. She had the power to cut off his air. She could do it.

But she didn't.

She kept wrapping.

Layer after layer until his head looked twice the size it used to.

"It'f hawtf in here! I can barry breaph!"

"Shut the fuck up," Mary said. "Shut the fuck up and listen."

She put her hands on Gilbert's shoulders and massaged them. She could feel his muscles relax as she inched up from his shoulders to his neck. She made sure to apply an intimidating amount of pressure there.

"You've changed, Gil. We don't talk anymore. You don't smile. It's all about fucking tuna sandwiches and pickles and the next dead fucking loser on our driveway. I can't take it anymore."

She smacked the side of his head. He didn't say ouch or fuck or get up to beat her. She wrapped too many layers around his head. He hardly felt it.

"I can't talk fru thifh!"

"Shut up!"

Mary wrapped a layer around Gilbert's neck and playfully tugged him backwards in his chair.

"Imagine what I could do," she said and tugged harder.

He coughed through the bandages.

"Mary, pleasuh stop!"

"Shut up!" she smacked on his head and when he didn't react, again, she slapped him as hard as she could on his bare back.

"Fuck!"

"Shut up and listen!" Mary said. "I'm not making any lunch for us today. We're taking the car and we're going to get chicken nuggets. Remember when we used to eat chicken nuggets in your old car? We'd walk through parks, french fries and chicken nuggets and chocolate shakes? Remember that? What happened to that Gil? What happened to us, Gil?"

Gilbert slouched in the chair.

Mary began unraveling the extra and unnecessary layers around his head.

As soon as the bandages were out of his mouth, Gilbert said, "Fine. You need to drive though. I had too much rum. And be fucking careful. My car is a moving death trap, now."

Mary kissed him on the cheek and got the keys.

***

"How's Larry?" Mary asked as she started the car. She didn't notice the puddle of blood Gilbert was sitting in or the puddle of blood in the backseat.

"He's, uh, okay," Gilbert said. He tried sitting as stiff as he could, not wanting to set off any of the reverse guillotines he had set up.

"Just okay? A few days ago he was slobbering all over himself!"

"Just keep your eyes on the road and sit very, very still, darling," Gilbert said, afraid to even reach for his seat belt in feat that he might lose his arm.

"It drives so well, Gil!" she bounced in her seat. "Just like old times." She turned to Gil, who was motionless. If she could see his face, she'd see him practically crying in fear, but he was bandaged up and the propane accident had burned out his tear ducts. Oh, well.

"I'm telling you, darling. Be careful!"

"You're such a worry wart!"

"Welcome to McDonalds," the loudspeaker at the drive through squawked. "How may I take your order?"

"Two six piece nuggets, two medium fries, and two chocolate shakes."

"Ma'am," the loudspeaker sounded, "Did you know you could get a twenty piece chicken nugget order for just $4.99? You'd save fifty cents and get more."

Mary turned to Gilbert, a smile as wide as the horizon.

"That's value," she said before turning back toward the loudspeaker. "We'll take it!"

She leaned over the power window and said, "and make those two large chocolate shakes!"

Gilbert grabbed her shoulder and pulled her back into the car.

"Do not, I repeat, do not put your head over the barrier. I swear to God almighty, you have no idea what this car is capable of now."

She smacked Gilbert on the leg.

"Oh, shut up! You're just paranoid!"

"Do you see the puddle of blood I'm sitting in? Do you see the puddle of blood in the backseat?"

"Ma'am?"

"I guess I glanced right over them!"

"Ma'am?"

"Yes, what is it?" Mary answered.

"Does this complete your order?"

"It does! Thank you!"

"Please pull up to the second window."

They did.

The teenager behind the window smiled as she held out her hand for Mary's money. Mary dug through her purse.

"You're going to have to lean in a little bit more, sweetie," Gilbert said to the worker from the passenger seat. "We may not look it, but we're a little old. A little bit older than you. Not much but, eh, you know. A little bit more."

The teenager smiled and put her hand closer. Mary dumped a twenty dollar bill in her hand.

"Keep the change, sweetheart," Mary said and patted the teenager's hand. "Nobody should be subjected to my husband's flirting without a little compensation."

"Ma'am," the teen said, "I can't take tips. It's against the rules." She handed a bag of fries and the chicken nuggets to Mary.

"Mary, be careful!" Gilbert said.

"I insist," Mary said, "I insist!"

"It's very nice but it isn't worth losing my job over," the teen said and tried to give Mary her change.

"How rude!" Mary yelled. "I want to see a manager!"

"Bitch, you ain't going to see no manager. Now take this fucking change. I don't need that money!"

Mary leaned through the window to grab the change. As she leaned, her necklace got caught underneath the power windows button and pulled at it.

The blade came fast and Mary's head popped into the teenager's hands.

The teen screamed and dropped Mary's head. As she screamed, her co-workers came by and each of them dropped everything they were doing and screamed, too. French fries fell, cheeseburgers fell, chocolate shakes — in fact, Gilbert's and Mary's chocolate shakes — fell and coated the room in blood and food. Mary's neck arteries were still active on both sides. Her body in the driver's seat of the car pumped blood and her head that was being kicked around accidentally on the kitchen floor was pumping a healthy amount of blood, coating the workers and the food. Customers spilled out of the McDonalds, climbing, falling, and running over each other as fast as they could. Kids were screaming, customers — who probably hadn't even seen the carnage — were screaming because everyone else was. It was a clusterfuck.

Gilbert sat in the passenger side of his car. The screams echoed and bounced around in his head. He looked forward to the empty lot that used to be a gas station. A bunch of hoodlums congregated there to drink out of brown paper bags and deal drugs.

"You killed Mary," he told them. "You killed Mary."

He turned to the teenager who wouldn't take a tip. She was still standing in place. Screaming, her hands at her face as Mary's unseen head pumped more blood onto the poor girl. Gilbert didn't even see her crying.

"You should have taken the fucking tip," he said.

The girl didn't respond.

He turned back to the hoodlums.

"You killed Mary."

Gilbert waited at the front of the drive through. He didn't take off his seatbelt. He stayed in the passenger seat. Mary's headless body accompanied. By the time the police showed up, the entire McDonalds was empty. Everyone had gone home sick except for the manager who was obviously in over his head. He stared at Gilbert through the drive thru window with his hands on his hips. He shook his head as he changed his gaze from the blood all over the place to Gilbert sitting like a statue in the car. He had gel in his hair and sweat stains on his pits. He still had his drive through intercom headphones on his head.

Bob O walked to the passenger side of Gilbert's car.

"Dammit, Gil," he said as he chewed some gum. "When I said to make it cleaner, I didn't mean this. I meant nothing, no body, no blood, just disappearance."

"Bob O, do not," Gilbert said, "I repeat, do not lean through my window unless you want to lose your head. This whole fucking car is booby-trapped."

"Jesus Christ," Bob O said. "Get out of the car. You going to eat those french fries?"

Gilbert unbuckled and opened the door. He got out, wobbly from his waning drunkenness, with the bag of fries and chicken nuggets in his hand.

"You going to eat those?" Bob O asked again.

Gilbert dropped them to the floor.

"Fucking asshole," Bob O said as he bent over to grab the bag. He pulled out some fries and stuffed them in his mouth.

"All right, all right, you're here. The McDonalds employee pulls a gun on you, your death trap malfunctions and kills your wife instead of the suspect who has conveniently escaped," Bob O nodded as the words fell out of his mouth. He licked the salt off his fingers and grabbed for more fries.

"That's not what happened at all," the manager said.

"Who the fuck is talking to you? I'll get your statement after I'm done working out his," Bob O said. He dug through the bag. "Look at this, would you look at this?" He grabbed the manager by the tie and pulled his face into the bag of food. "Only two packets of barbecue sauce for twenty nuggets? What the hell is this shit? No wonder this poor lady lost her fucking head. Give me three more or I'm booking you for being uncooperative with an officer of the law!"

Gilbert wasn't paying attention. His gaze was focused on the hoodlums across the street. They squatted, spat, and smoked as they laid out dollar bills and played dice.

"Here's what happened," Bob O said, "your wife, in anger, fought with you over the cost of the meal. You, the frugal son of a bitch that you are, said you should have just gotten one large order of fries and shared. She, always kind of on the weighty side, protested. The argument got so heated that she revealed to you that this whole car was a death trap of her making and she was going to kill you both. She accidentally only killed herself. Shit happens."

The manager interrupted Bob O with a whole bag of BBQ sauce. Bob O thanked him and opened five packets, dedicating a nugget per packet.

"Say whatever you need to say," Gilbert said. "All of this is my fault. I shouldn't have let her drive. We should have moved to the country and ran us a farm. Instead, I took her to the suburbs where a bunch of fucking punks like that – " Gilbert pointed to the guys across the street at the abandoned gas station, "can do whatever they want. There's no fear. No retribution. The police can't go a full fucking second without stuffing some chicken nugget down their throats. What is it with you people?"

Bob O dipped his pointer finger into a packet of BBQ sauce and licked it.

"You know, Gil, for a guy who's getting my help, you sure sound like a whiny bitch. Why is it that McDonalds BBQ sauce only tastes good with McDonalds nuggets? Why can't you get a Chick-Fil-A nugget and dunk it in some good ol' Mickey D's sauce? I don't get it but it's true."

"Is that what you think about all fucking day?" Gilbert got in Bob O's face. "My wife's dead because I had to go to some pretty extreme measures to clean up this bankrupt, good for nothing town and you're here talking about the compatibility of barbecue sauces with competing brands' nuggets?" Gilbert stepped away and pointed at the hoodlums across the street. "Arrest them!"

"For what?"

"Killing Mary!"

"They didn't kill Mary. You killed Mary," Bob O said as he licked his fingers clear of any trace of meal.

"No, Bob O, no." Gilbert marched up to Bob O and stuck his finger into Bob O's chest. "You killed Mary."

There was silence as the two men stared at each other, fuming.

"Yo, is this guy even a cop?" the manager, who had all but been forgotten by Bob O and Gilbert, asked.

Bob O, with his eyes still on Gilbert, grabbed the manager's head and struck it down on the metal casing of the order window.

"You're definitely under arrest for non-compliance," Bob O said as the body slumped out of view. "We're going with the fight over the cost of the meal story. You'll be fine. No one's going to jail. I've farted out worse stories than that and still got my way. We're going to have to tow the car to the department. I'll give you a ride home. In the meantime, stay out of Cliff's until you've come up with a cleaner method of kill. Now, get in my car. You're going to go home and you're going to grieve, motherfucker."

***

An empty bottle of whiskey sat at Gilbert's nightstand. He cradled another close to his chest as he sat in bed with a hand on the void Mary would have filled. He couldn't cry. There was still trash to take out. Any hint of any of this being Gilbert's fault was drowned out by the roar of alcohol he poured down his throat.

It was seven in the morning. In two minutes, his alarm would go off. Fully awake, he waited for it.

As soon as it went off, so did he. He grabbed the alarm clock and pulled it out of the wall. He threw it against the wall and charged it as it hit the floor. He stomped on it.

"Fuck you! Fuck you! Fuck you!"

His doorbell rang.

"Go away!"

The doorbell rang again.

"Get the fuck out of here!"

They rang the doorbell and knocked at the same time.

Gilbert glugged down some more whiskey and poured what remained on the shattered and in pieces clock. He walked down the hall. As he passed the fridge, he pulled out a beer and drank as he stumbled for the door.

"Who the fuck is it?!"

"Hey, uh, Gil," Larry's dumb voice sounded from behind the closed door.

"What?! What?" Gilbert kicked the door to punctuate his screaming.

"Bernadette is taking this pretty hard, blaming me and shit... you know. You think I can lay low here for a few days?"

Gilbert rolled his eyes and unchained the door.

"You better have some fucking liquor or you'll be hanging out with the ghosts in the shed."

Larry came in. He had a grocery bag with two bottles of rum and a six pack of beer. He smiled.

"Sorry for your loss, Gil," he said.

"Only Mary can call me Gil."

"I know, I just thought that maybe... you know. You'd like to hear a familiar voice say a familiar thing?"

Gilbert whacked him across the head.

"Open the bottle of rum," he said. His bandages were old with his own blood and Mary's blood from the day before. There was no one anymore to change them for him. He didn't want them changed. Their blood would carry out vengeance, sweat through the night like the old times, and mix forever and ever, amen.

His face was clammier with sweat this morning. Not sleeping had taken a toll on him. He could feel the pus in his scabs leak out onto the other scabs and tear away from his skin. Every movement, no matter how small, sent an ache all over.

"Geez, Gil. You know – " Larry took a sip of his bottle of rum, "I'd've thought your bandages would be off by now. Hasn't your face healed at all?"

"Shut up," Gilbert said. "Your wife kicked you out because you're a pussy. Too afraid to do what has to be done to clean up this town."

"She's blaming me for Mary's death."

"Does she have any reason not to?"

Larry got quiet. His hands trembled with the bottle of rum as he sipped again, spilling some on his shirt.

"Look at you. You're about to piss your pants," Gilbert said. "I'm not going to kill you. Just know that I know when the war came to your garden, you cowered and cried and surrendered."

Gilbert chuckled and poured nearly a quarter of the bottle of rum down his throat.

"I can stay somewhere else, Gil," Larry said. He looked at the carpet where he sat.

His eyes didn't dare catch the gaze of Gilbert's sunglasses.

"Stay here. Stay here. Please. I need the company of a quivering pussy tonight."

Gilbert grabbed a beer and chugged it.

"You don't have to be so mean, you know?"

Gilbert spit the beer out of his mouth and through his nose laughing.

"Who's being mean, you son of a bitch? Who?" Gilbert stood up. His belly hung out of his halfway buttoned shirt as he chugged the rest of the beer. He turned to look at Larry, Larry who was still not looking anywhere near Gilbert's direction. "Look at me," Gilbert said. "Look at me and hear this. There's a war outside. The police are too underfunded to help. The schools are too underfunded to get any of their kids to college and thus we have a generation of criminals we need to take out. You were a willing partner until some dead guy shit all over himself in your driveway. When it happened in my driveway, it was okay. You'll be cleaning up the bloodstains whether you're with me or not! So look at me, goddamn you!"

Larry didn't look up. He sobbed into his knees and said nothing.

Gilbert grabbed him by the collar and threw him off his couch. Larry tumbled to the floor. Gilbert had his empty beer bottle in hand and knocked it against Larry's head.

"Jesus Christ, Gil!"

Gilbert grabbed the beer bottle again and whacked it against Larry's face. Larry's nose was bleeding, his nostrils were just skin flaps that fluttered with each gush of blood coming out of them.

"Only Mary can call me Gil and she's dead, motherfucker!"

Gilbert grabbed him by the collar and dragged him across the linoleum floor. This, too, reminded Gilbert of Mary and how she always wanted to put in wood flooring. He could have done it, too, if he'd saved the money he put into his death machines.

"This is all your fault," Gilbert said in his violent trance. "Look at these fucking floors! You can see the purple stains where water pipes burst decades ago. It's cracking and tearing and they could have been fucking wood!"

"Wh-wh-what the fuck are you talking about?"

Larry wriggled as his ass dragged from the living room to the kitchen.

"You're a coward," Gilbert said. "There's no room for cowards in this town anymore. You see a problem and you fucking fix it. You're the problem now."

Gilbert grabbed Larry's neck and tightened his grip. With his free hand he opened the oven door and turned on the heat.

"You're gonna get Plath'd."

Gilbert shoved Larry's head into the oven. Larry screamed and writhed out of Gilbert's grip. One punch made Gilbert stumble away long enough for Larry to stare him in the eyes and run away.

"Run! Run! That's all you're good for anyway!"

Larry ran out the front door, leaving it open, and the morning sun burned Gilbert's face and caused his scabs to itch. His bandages were coming unraveled but Gilbert didn't notice. He went to the door and locked it. He stuck a chair underneath the door handle in case anyone tried to come in.

Gilbert opened another beer and sat on his couch. He turned on the TV and let the commercials of used car salesmen lull him to sleep.

Yelling from Larry's house woke him up. He got up and opened the blinds to the side window facing Larry's house. It didn't help him hear what they were fighting about any better but it helped him focus on their argument without any visual disruptions.

"You're a pussy!"

"Fuck you!"

And then there was a gunshot and the screaming stopped.

"Oh, shit," Gilbert said to himself and closed the blinds as fast as he could. He sat back in his chair and turned the TV volume up, holding the remote control in his hand like a weapon or a believable enough excuse of ignorance.

He heard the front door slam. Bernadette's silhouette struggled as she dragged something across Gilbert's lawn and into his side lawn. Gilbert stood up.

"Get off my lawn!"

The silhouette stopped. Gilbert could see clearly that she was flipping him off and then continued to drag Larry's body. Gilbert stayed put on his couch and turned the volume up even more. On her way back, Bernadette stopped at the front window again. She was yelling but Gilbert couldn't hear it. She started to smear blood on the window.

You clean him up

Then Bernadette moved on and went back into her house and there was another shot gun blast.

Gilbert jumped out of his chair and put on his shoes. He ran for the garage, opened it, and ran out. His car was still in police possession so he walked to Cliff's. La Palma is only a square mile all around, it wouldn't take long.

***

"Here comes the peanut stealer," Bob O said as he filled his mouth with peanuts.

Gilbert walked straight for his table and took a seat.

Bob O motioned to the folks sitting with him for them to leave and they did.

"I've got big problems," Gilbert said. His face was half exposed, the walk made him sweat most the bandages off and his scabs had reopened and started dribbling blood.

"Yeah, me too," Bob O smiled. "I've gotta clean up your mess all over town."

"I'm cleaning up the mess all over town. You're tying up loose ends."

Bob O grabbed the pitcher of beer between them and poured a glass for Gilbert.

"Think of any ways to clean up your process?"

"Yeah, yeah. Gas. I stuck Larry's head in the oven and realized gas killing is the cleanest method available."

"Hmmm..." Bob O sucked the beer foam out of his mustache. "Takes too long. Did you kill him?"

"He got away. His wife shot him, probably killed herself too from what I heard."

"We keep cleaning the town up like this, there'll be no town left."

"You're saying *we* like you've got anything to do with anything so far."

Bob O got up and threw a twenty on the table.

"No gas. I know a guy who works in executions at the penitentiary. Lethal injections. That's the way to go."

Gilbert looked up.

"Clean yourself up. The La Palma Police is looking for a driver for our new fleet of MEVs."

"MEVs?"

"Mobile Execution Vehicles. We'll supply the vans and the lethal injection juice. You just drive around and respond to our calls. Nobody will know a damn thing."

Bob O stuck his hand out for a handshake.

"Are you in?"

Gilbert nodded and shook Bob O's hand.

"You've just been deputized. We'll drop off the keys and the van tomorrow morning. Get some rest and clean yourself up."

Andrew Hilbert

GEORGE

Death Thing

"Those damn kids are at it again," George said, his eyes peeking through the blinds of his living room window.

"Well, go out there and shoo them off!" said his wife, Martha.

"They've got rocks, Martha! What if they throw them at me and split my goddamn head open?"

"Call the police then!"

Martha was spraying Windex on the mirrors around the house. She could care less about kids with rocks so long as the rocks didn't go through the windows she just cleaned.

"I should. Damn kids'll hurt themselves."

George picked up the phone that he left on the ground next to his beer cooler and the La-Z-Boy recliner he called his. He dialed 9-1-1.

"La Palma Police Department. Is this an emergency?" a bored, female voice answered.

"It may damn well turn into one."

"What is it, sir?"

"Get a police car out here to take care of these damn kids throwing rocks at each other."

"We'll have an officer out there shortly."

"Thanks."

"Sir, for future reference, these kinds of calls can be directed to our non-emergency line."

George hung up the phone and peeked out the window. He lowered the TV volume because it helped him concentrate on watching the kids and their impending punishment.

Not five minutes passed before a police car drove down the street.

"5-0!" one kid yelled and dove into George's flower bed, right in front of the window. The other kids scattered and ran away.

"Little shit," George said to himself. He got up and went to his front yard. The cop stood, hands on his waist, outside his car writing something down and talking into his radio.

"Howdy, officer," George said.

"Damn kids are too fast for me," he slapped his hands against his pot belly. George could see his white undershirt underneath his buttons. "I figure seeing me is a good enough scare for a few days. You call us back if they're back, though. We'll take care of 'em."

George inched closer to the officer and said, in a very low voice, "One of those fuckers is hiding in my flower bed." George pointed with his nose to the flower bed.

"Yeah?" the officer said and chewed a little more enthusiastically on his gum. "Bring out the MEV," he said into his radio then turned back to George. "Go inside, sir. That kid's in for a good surprise. The other kids may be back but this one won't be, heh-heh."

"Thanks," George walked back to the front steps of his house and did his best not to tip off the little shit hiding in his flowers.

"Kid's in for a surprise," George said as he entered his house.

"What?" Martha yelled over the rumble of her vacuum cleaner.

"Kid's in for a – never mind," George climbed back into his recliner and peeked out his blinds again, salivating revenge.

An unmarked Econoline van parked in front of the house. The driver rolled down his window. The cop pointed to the flower bed and, as soon as he did that, three men in white lab coats popped out the back of the van and rushed the garden.

The look of terror on the kid's eyes was so perfect that George smiled and popped open a beer.

"They're really cracking down on these shits," he said and took a sip. "That kid is scared as hell. Almost thought he could make a good actor 'til I realized he wasn't acting."

The lab coats had the kid by the arms. He was wriggling and screaming and crying.

"I want my mom!" George heard him yell. George smiled and took another sip.

"I sure hope mommy's a lawyer," George said to himself, laughed, and turned up the volume. The lab coats threw the kid into the back of the van and drove off.

"Martha! God dammit! Can't you vacuum tomorrow when I'm at work and won't be bothered by that damn death hum vacuum!"

"What?" Martha yelled, her back was to George because she vacuumed walking backward so that footsteps didn't show up in the carpet when she was done.

"Exactly," George took another sip and stared at the TV. "Alex Trebek has aged well," he thought to himself.

***

The next day, kids were out again throwing rocks at each other. They laughed and jumped and yelled out in pain every now and then, but mostly they were laughing.

George had a hangover that felt like Whack-a-Mole in his head and he'd had the shittiest day of his life cleaning up the restrooms at Costco.

"God damn little shits," George said. "Can't a working man get a little peace?"

Their laughter was continuous and banged at his brain like a mallet handled by a sadist. George picked up the phone, tried to remember the non-emergency number, but ended up dialing 9-1-1 anyway.

"La Palma Police Department. What's the emergency?"

The lady's boredom was antidote to the kids' laughter.

"Yeah, those damn kids are back throwing rocks at each other and if one of them dies on my lawn, I'm burying them all in it!"

"Mr. Sanders?"

"Yes?"

"We'll send out an MEV immediately. You can call the non-emergency line if it happens again."

George hung up and watched out his window as another unmarked Econoline van pulled up. The kids had no idea that it was a police vehicle. Three lab coats hopped out of the back of the van and chased one, just one, kid around until they caught him and threw him into the back of the van and drove off.

"They can fit twenty scab lickers in that god damn thing!" George yelled.

The kids that were left looked at each other in real terror, dropped their rocks, and ran home.

"Did the trick, though." George leaned back in his recliner, reached for a beer, and took a gulp. "Ahhh," he said.

Martha started up with the vacuum and George felt like his brain was growing tumors.

"God dammit, Martha!" George yelled.

"What?"

"Do you need to vacuum every single day!?"

"What?"

***

The next day, there were only three kids playing outside. They were skateboarding and, of course, throwing rocks at each other whenever one of them wanted to show off. The kids were more violent today than other days. George was glad to see their ranks thinning. A ride in the police van was enough to scare them back to their toilets.

George peeked out of his windows and watched. He decided not to call the police but as soon as one of the kids saw him, they started throwing rocks at George's house.

"God dammit!" George grabbed his phone and dialed 9·1·1 on instinct.

"Mr. Sanders?" the lady answered.

"Yes! Send out the police. The kids are throwing rocks at my property!"

"We'll send an MEV. Next time, call the non·emergency line. Do you have a pen and paper? I can give it to you righ·" but George hung up, lay flat on his stomach, and covered his head. The rocks hit the window hard and glass shattered all over the carpet.

Martha wasn't slow in responding, she turned the vacuum right on.

"Not now, Martha!" George yelled.

Suddenly, the rocks stopped.

"Oh, shit!" yelled one of the kids and George got up to see. "It's the Death Thing!"

The kids scattered but as soon as they did, two more Econoline vans showed up and nine lab coats chased three kids until they were all caught and crying and thrown into the back of each one of them. The vans sped off.

George smiled but if the MEVs were as effective as they'd proven to be, he knew he'd never get the $200 to fix his window. That was worth it, though. $200 was worth a little peace.

***

A few days passed and there were no kids playing, laughing, screaming, throwing rocks, or breaking things. It was nice. George drank his beer in his recliner, admired Alex Trebek's cocky intellect, and yelled at Martha while she vacuumed. He could say whatever he wanted while she did it, so he did knowing that she would just reply with, "What?"

She didn't vacuum today though. She brought out the morning paper.

"George, did you see this?" she threw the paper on George's lap.

Five kids' faces were on the front page with a huge headline that said: MISSING.

They were the kids George had the police chase out of town.

"Holy cow," George said to himself and peeked out the window. The streets were empty. George was the kind of guy that was only happy when he was unhappy and the past three days were eerie without any kids to complain about.

Then it hit him.

"One of the kids called the police van a death thing when they showed up last time..." George said.

"Kids'll say anything! The police probably just drove them home. They were naughty kids. I wouldn't be surprised if they died in a heroin den."

"These kids were twelve, Martha."

"They start so young these days," Martha shook her head, turned away from George, and turned on the vacuum. She walked backward, erasing her footsteps as she worked. Sometimes she hummed and tried to harmonize with the vacuum's scream.

"You're an idiot," George said to Martha's back.

"What?" she answered and started to harmonize with the atonal machine.

George picked up the phone and dialed 9-1-1.

"La Palma Police Department. What's the emergency?"

"Hey, I just have a question," George said.

"Sir, you can dial the non-emergency line!" the voice was no longer bored but exasperated and irritated.

"Just what does MEV stand for?"

"Mr. Sanders! It's the model of van the Department purchased in bulk from Ford. All non-emergency calls should be directed to our non-emergency line!"

George hung up and peeked outside the window. An unmarked Econoline van was parked outside his house.

"Huh?" George opened his blinds completely and watched as the driver, in police uniform, got out of the car and talked into his radio as he walked to the front door.

The doorbell rang.

"What?" said Martha.

George got up and opened the door.

"What is it, officer?"

"Sir, we've received many complaints of you abusing the 9·1·1 emergency call system. I'll need to take you in."

"This is ridiculous. Who complained?!"

"We complained, sir."

"What the hell does MEV stand for?"

"It's the model of Econoline van that we had specially modified for incarcerations. I'll need you to turn around so I can handcuff you."

George turned around. Martha was totally unaware of what was happening. Her back was turned to the door and she was humming over the vacuum cleaner.

"Martha! Martha!" George yelled as the officer cuffed him.

"What?"

"Jesus friggin' Christ, Martha! Stop vacuuming!" George yelled.

Three lab coats got out of the back of the van and assisted the officer in dragging George into it.

First thing they did was strap George's head down on a plastic stretcher so that it couldn't move a single millimeter to either side. George felt claustrophobic as he watched the ceiling of the perfectly white interior of the van. He couldn't see the lab coat's faces so he continued to yell.

"Martha! Martha!"

Then they strapped his arms and legs to the stretcher. The back door of the van shut and the van started driving.

"Martha!"

"George Sanders, do you understand the charges leveled against you?" said one of the lab coats.

"I have no fucking clue what was leveled against me!"

"Mr. Sanders, by the power vested in me by the laws of the California government and the incorporated city of La Palma, I declare you guilty of criminal misconduct and abuse of the 9-1-1 emergency call system."

"What!?"

One lab coat made sure to put the needle the size of a garden hose right into George's line of sight.

"What's that for!?"

George felt the cold needle go into his arm. He was paralyzed. Another lab coat lifted another needle to George's line of sight. George couldn't scream or ask questions.

It went into his other arm and he felt like he had no body at all. He was getting drowsy, his eyes heavier with each blink. A third needle went in and that was that.

Andrew Hilbert

GIL

Death Thing

It was hot in the van.

It was stripped down, with none of the amenities you'd expect in a van that was "brand new" to the police force.

Brand new meant different things. Brand new to an orphan is just a pair of worn out Nikes a kid dumped in a donation box thinking it was a dumpster in the grocery store parking lot.

The heater was non-functioning. AC wasn't even an option. There was a hole where a radio was pried out and probably sold for ten dollars worth of crack.

"Jesus fucking Christ," Gilbert said as he turned the key and started the van.

There was a cup holder, though. That was good because Gilbert was drinking non-stop these days. Being deputized wasn't enough to fill the Mary-sized hole in his heart.

Gilbert dropped a six pack in the passenger seat and drove around. He was waiting for a call, a call to duty. Bob O had an 80s car phone installed in the center console. It was slightly smaller than Gilbert's face.

"This is what my tax dollars fucking pay for," Gilbert said to himself. He was what his tax dollars paid for, too.

Gilbert took in the sights. He still wasn't sure how proactive he should be in his new assignment.

Two kids loitering underneath a clearly marked NO LOITERING sign outside the 7-11. An old lady jaywalking. A dog pooping on someone's lawn. They were all as good as dead to Gilbert. None of their lives meant a damn thing anymore.

Gilbert stayed away from the McDonald's.

"All calls involving McDonald's should be redirected to somebody else," Gilbert told Bob O when the keys were first handed to him. It would be too painful to revisit the scene where Mary's head became separated from Mary's body.

The phone rang. It was loud and the sound banged around the sparse interior of the MEV. Gilbert could feel his wounds opening again underneath his bandages with each vibration.

"What?" he answered.

"That's no way to speak to your superior, deputy," Bob O's voice, punctuated with the sound of crunching peanuts, said on the other end.

"Yeah, fuck off." Gilbert hung up the phone and returned to driving.

The phone rang again. This time some of the bandages fell off where they were held up by Gilbert's own dried blood.

Gilbert didn't say anything when he answered.

"I can hear breathing," Bob O said. "So I'm going to assume you're listening."

Gilbert nodded as if Bob O could see him.

"We need you at the 7-11. Two kids are loitering and harassing adults to buy them beer. Loitering leads to looting which leads to murder. These kids have no excuse, Gil."

"Don't call me Gil," Gilbert said and hung up. At the stop light he did an illegal U-turn and doubled back toward the 7-11 where he had initially spotted the pimply faced freaks committing heinous misdemeanors.

He popped open his can of beer and chugged it. He left the car running in the parking lot as he got out of the van.

"Wow, look at that fuckin' thing, man!" one of the teenagers pointed at Gilbert's face.

"He looks like fuckin' death, man."

"Hey, death thing! You wanna buy us some beer? We got five bucks."

"Grandpa probably wants a blow job."

The kids laughed and pointed.

"No, but, seriously, man. We just want some beer."

Gilbert grimaced. He could feel his infected wounds opening. He could feel the yellow pus and red blood dripping down his cheeks.

"Woah, man, gross. This guy is death, man."

"I wouldn't suck his dick even if his dick spewed beer, man."

"You won't be sucking anyone's dick." Gilbert grabbed one of the teenagers by the ear and damn near pulled it off as he dragged the kid to the back of the MEV. He opened the trunk and threw him in.

One amenity the force didn't skimp on was the child lock doors.

Gilbert slammed the trunk doors closed and watched the other teenager shit himself.

"You going to run? You going to make this harder for us than it has to be?" Gilbert took out his wallet and showed the kid his photocopied picture of a badge.

"You think that fuckin' thing scares me, man? My dad's a fucking lawyer!"

Gilbert pointed at the pile of diarrhea that was amassing under the pant leg of the kid.

"I think this thing scares you quite a bit, son. Get in the fucking van and we'll sort this out at the station."

"Y-y-yes, sir."

"Don't start crying, you little bitch."

Gilbert led the unrepentant loiterer to the back side of the MEV, opened the trunk, and said, "Ladies first."

When it got down to it, the kid was pretty damn obedient. He put his head down and hopped in, trying to conceal his sobbing the whole time.

Gilbert slammed the trunk door and headed back for the driver's seat. He got in the car and threw them two beers. "You should know, kids, that drinking underage is a crime. You should also know that these beers are your last so drink up."

Gilbert watched them in his rearview mirror. They didn't open the beers. They just set them aside and trembled.

Bob O offered Gilbert an assistant but Gilbert refused. He worked alone. The closest things he had to assistants were dead now. No use in condemning another noble civil servant to the same fate.

"New La Palma Police Department policy I have to tell you kids about," Gilbert said. "We give everyone tetanus shots before processing. Blame it on the Democrats."

He pulled up to the police station parking lot and parked. This time he took the keys out and made his way back to the back of the van. When he opened the trunk, the two teenagers were trembling in each other's embrace.

"Ah, fuck." Gilbert closed the trunk again and walked into the station.

"Good morning, Gil," Janice, the secretary who put on too much lipstick, said to him as he strolled into the office.

"Where's Bob O?"

"Doing what he normally does in his office. Lord knows what." Janice made the sign of the cross and looked to the popcorn ceiling for guidance.

"I'm going back there."

"Gil, Gil!" Janice yelled as Gilbert walked past. "He said no interruptions!"

Gilbert stopped mid stride and turned around. She ran right into him.

"Janny, my dear, if you call me Gil one more time I'm going to burn this fucking place to the ground."

Janice nodded and ran back to her desk.

Bob O was napping at his desk.

"Wake up, you fat waste of money."

"What the hell is it, Gil?"

"I don't like the cleanliness of this whole operation. I can't stick kids with needles. There has to be more."

"You got the loiterers on city property?" Bob O stood up. "Where the fuck are they? Where in the goddamn fuck are they?"

"Relax, they're in the back of the MEV."

"Don't ever bring bodies back here again."

"They're alive."

"Going soft?" Bob O sat back down and kicked his legs up on his desk. "Peanut?" He pointed to a jar of peanuts.

"No."

"Don't sweat it. My nephew is here today. Shadowing us. Seeing what it's like to be a man of the law. I'll get him to vaccinate those turds." Bob O pushed a button on his phone. "Janice, bring Eric to me."

In seconds, Eric was there.

"Yes, Uncle Bobby?"

Bob O pointed to Gilbert. "This is Gil. He needs you for some cleanup work."

Eric nodded. He couldn't be any older than the teenagers in the van.

"As you know, new La Palma Police Department policy is to vaccinate every person we pick up for tetanus. Gil here has got a thing with needles, so he needs you to do it for him."

"The injections are in a briefcase in the glove box of the white van parked outside. You can do it yourself, kid," Gilbert said.

"Sir, yes, sir!" Eric saluted and ran off.

"That fucking twerp a military reject or something?"

"What gave it away?" Bob O grabbed a handful of peanuts and shoved them in his mouth. "By the way, Gil," Bob O said with peanuts falling out of his mouth, "you gotta rewrap your head or something. It's getting gross."

"There's nobody to do it for me anymore."

***

At night, Gilbert took a drive around the block before he got home to patrol the streets of the neighborhood that he made safer. There was nothing unusual anymore. Kids didn't play outside like they used to.

Gilbert smiled through his bandages. He could be proud of his work.

When he got home, the house was dark and empty. The familiar sound of something frying didn't greet him as he walked in. He didn't bother turning on any lights. He preferred the darkness.

He grabbed a frozen dinner out of the freezer and popped it in the microwave. Two minutes and thirty seconds.

For two minutes and thirty seconds, he stared at his meal rotating in the glow of the radiation. The microwave beeped and he grabbed it. He sat on his reclining chair and stared at the TV. The TV wasn't on.

Halfway through his meal, he set it down and got up.

"I'm just stepping out for a bit, hon," he said out of habit.

He took a walk to the few doors down where he and Larry had stuffed one of his first victims into a trunk. It was still there, unnoticed, judging by the flies.

"Fucking memory lane," Gilbert said to himself. The gate on the side of the house was left open, as it always was. And, as he always did, he walked right through it.

He knew where he was going. He had his eyes on the woman who still lived with her parents. She was up to something, sure. He wasn't sure what it was but he was sure she belonged in the MEV.

There was a blue glow emanating from the window. She kept her blinds up.

"Exhibitionist," Gilbert said. He watched her sleeping through the window. She was fast asleep; eyes closed, the flicker of the commercials projecting onto her skin, totally unaware that a man with an infected face was staring at her, waiting for his turn to take her call with the MEV.

After a few minutes, the bandages on Gilbert's face started to fall. He never could wind them as tight as Mary did. They scraped and irritated him as they blew in the wind.

It was time to go home. There was still a half-eaten frozen dinner to eat at home, alone.

***

"Got another call for ya, Gil."

"Bob O, you might be a fan of stupid nicknames but I'm not. Stop calling me Gil or you'll be the next up for a tetanus shot."

"Relax, relax. You know, if you don't like this job we've got three other vans running twenty-four seven around town. We gave this MEV to you to honor your commitment to safer streets."

Gilbert didn't respond. He pulled the tab on another beer and started to sip.

"You there?"

"I'm listening."

Gilbert hung a photo of Mary when she was younger on his rearview mirror. He kept his eyes on it. She was his protector. He was too weak to protect her.

"You catch that?"

"You were talking?"

"Jesus Christ, Gil, clean out your goddamn ears or go to a doctor and get your face disinfected. It's really starting to affect our relationship."

Gilbert said nothing.

Death Thing

Andrew Hilbert

Joey

&

Cheese

Death Thing

Joey lit her joint as she steered with her left knee. She did her best to keep one eye on the road and another on her lighter but depth perception is all off when you're not looking with both. She was either close to burning off her nose or burning her thumb because the lighter was on for too long and heated the sparker, leaving the joint perpetually unlit.

"Just fucking pullover, man," Cheese said.

"You don't get to tell me how to drive when you're smoking my weed."

Cheese shrugged and turned up the radio.

"Police & Thieves, I love this song," he said.

Joey kept struggling with the lighter.

"Let me fucking light this thing. We're gonna get in an accident, man."

Joey passed the joint and lighter to Cheese.

"I gotta sell some weed to some assholes down at the abandoned gas station. Fuckers are probably going to want me to –" Joey swerved hard right to avoid a Chihuahua that had come unleashed from its owner. It ran into the street like an idiot. The owner shook his head.

"Get ahold of your fucking dog, man!" Joey yelled at the window, staring the guy down as she drove on. As soon as she put her eyes back on the road she had to slam on her brakes. There was a stop sign there. The stop sign didn't come out of nowhere. It was always there. But this time there was a black and white police car at the stop sign facing them, with a cop munching on donuts.

"You hear that sound from your trunk?" Cheese asked.

"What the fuck are you talking about?"

The police officer and Joey stared at each other, daring the other to go first. Joey and Cheese were already both high and they could stay there forever, not realizing how much time had passed before it was too late. The cop relented and drove off.

"You didn't hear that moving around?" Cheese asked and took a hit. "When you slammed on the brakes it sounded like something real heavy-like slammed against the front of the trunk and when you came to a stop it rolled back to the back of the trunk."

Joey took the joint from Cheese.

"You're fucking high, man."

"Police and thieves, bro," Cheese said and shook his head, "Police and fucking thieves. I don't care what anybody says. Whoever wrote this song is a fucking genius."

"Does anyone ever say anything?"

"What? Man, nah! I'm just saying!"

Joey nodded her head and put her foot on the gas. The growing line of cars stopped behind her was thankful.

***

They drove up to the abandoned gas station and Joey texted the kids she was supposed to meet. Joey tried to be at least 30 minutes late every deal. It showed people she didn't need their business and her time was precious. With these kids, though, she tried to be an hour late. They were usually the ones that were late and they weren't even there when Joey and Cheese rolled up.

"Fucking assholes," Joey said. "I swear to God that if I didn't have to save some money to get my trunk fixed, I'd never sell to these assholes again."

Cheese was sucking on what was left of the joint. His eyes were red and his blinking was getting heavier. Dried spit formed at the edges of his lips. He was going to need a soda, and quick.

"You ever think about the stars, man? You ever think about how we don't got 'em out here? I swear to God, man. I drove out for two hours, listenin' to Pink Floyd and shit and kept looking at the damn sky waiting to see more than the big fucking dipper. It never came. All that light pollution. Why we gotta do that?"

"What the fuck are you talking about?"

"Look up right now. There ain't a star in sight."

"It's daylight outside, Cheese."

"You're missing the point." Cheese shook his head, rolled down his window and threw the stub of the joint out. "We should have at least one day a year when everyone turns off their lights, all the city lights go off, all the billboard lights go off, all the McDonalds' sign lights go off, and everyone has a fucking picnic, gets high, and looks at the sky."

Cheese nodded, his eyes were closed, and he smiled as he got more lost in his thoughts.

"Yeah, man," he said. "Uh huh, I could really go for some french fries right about now."

Joey started the car again.

"Fuck these guys, let's go get chicken nuggets," she said.

"Yeah, man," Cheese mumbled. "Fucking chocolate shakes, too."

Joey drove off the empty lot and across the street to McDonalds. She parked and got out of the car. Cheese was paralyzed in his seat, eyes closed, and smiling.

"Man, why we not in the drive thru?"

"I want to waste time," Joey said. "Get your fat ass up and let's go."

"I shouldn't even be hanging with someone who's so mean to me," Cheese said. The combination of being high and overweight caused for more thought and struggle than usual to climb out of the car. "They better not charge extra for sweet and sour sauce for my fries. I fuckin' hate when they do that."

"Nothing's free, Cheese."

They walked to the front door. Cheese, a proper gentleman, held it open for the stream of folks leaving.

"Got here at the right time," Joey said. "Looks like we beat the rush."

"Fresh french fries. Won't have to worry about any soggy shit," Cheese said and chuckled.

Nobody was in line, nobody was sitting at a table. The McDonalds was uncharacteristically empty. They stood far enough from the counter to assure whoever was behind it that they were still hypnotized by the slew of options before them.

"I don't even know what I want anymore," Cheese said. He turned towards Joey whose gaze was still fixed on the menu. "I mean I know what I want but I know I can't have it."

"Get whatever you want," Joey said.

"What if I want everything?"

"Pare it down, then."

"How the fuck you think those wraps taste? I don't know how I feel about thousand island sauce in a tortilla."

"Probably tastes like microwaved throw up."

"I love thousand island sauce, though," Cheese said. "And I love tortillas."

"Then try it. Shit, nobody's going to kill you for trying fast food bullshit."

"But then again I kinda want some chicken nuggets. That guarantees to these motherfuckers that I get free sweet and sour sauce."

Joey crossed her arms and continued to stare at the menu.

"I think I know what I want."

"Yeah? What?"

"I don't know."

They both burst out laughing.

"Maybe we should go somewhere else," Joey said.

"Nah, fuck that. Once the cashier gets here, we'll know what we want."

They stepped forward a couple of paces and waited. Nobody was there to serve them. They didn't notice for a few minutes.

"I gotta get some drink in me before my mouth collapses on itself," Cheese said. "Cotton mouth like a motherfucker in here."

They stood in silence for a few more minutes.

"Fuck it," Cheese said. "I'm going to run my mouth under one of the fountains. I can't take this shit anymore."

"Go for water first. The syrup is just going to dry your mouth out more."

"You act like I've never been high before. Shit."

"Are we ever going to get any fucking service over here?" Joey leaned against the counter and yelled into the kitchen. Nobody answered.

"Hey, you!" she yelled at the manager at the window. "Why the hell aren't we being served?"

The manager looked at her and shook his head as if it was obvious to everyone why nobody was being served.

"Look, if I don't get a chocolate shake in two seconds I'm taking my business across the street!"

The manager ignored her. Cheese was slurping down root beer at the fountains. Joey walked to him and grabbed him by his hoodie.

"Let's go. Maybe those fucks are across the street."

"I got root beer all over my fucking face, man!"

"Whatever, wipe it off."

"You owe me," Cheese said. He took off his hoodie and wiped off his face. They walked outside toward the end of the drive thru.

"These fuckers are getting all the attention." Joey pointed to the car at the window. The manager was talking to them.

"Hey, yo, that bitch has no head, yo!" Cheese wiped his face again, to make sure he wasn't seeing with syrup eyes. "Yo, that bitch in the driver's seat has no fucking head!"

Joey looked at the car. Blood splattered in rhythmic increments onto the windshield.

"Holy shit," she said. "She has no head."

She looked at the passenger. It was her crotchety neighbor wearing bloodied bandages all over his head and sunglasses, looking across the street at her customers.

"We should get outta here," Joey said.

"What about Tweedle Dumb and Numb Nuts?" Cheese pointed across the street at the two idiots rolling dice.

"Fuck 'em," Joey said, "They can find a new dealer. That's my neighbor in that car. We gotta get outta here."

"Shit, I really coulda used some fries."

***

Joey lived with her parents. She started selling weed in college to pay for it but after college was done and seeing every job that would hire her as beneath her, she continued and made a decent living. Decent enough to pay for everything but rent. A degree in Art History allowed her to call herself an art historian, but didn't do much in the way of jobs. McDonalds was always hiring but people were always buying weed, too.

She and Cheese were known as a tag team. Cheese was like a brother to her and a son to her parents. Everyone knew what they were up to, nobody cared. Every now and then, her folks would sneak into her room and buy a gram and made Joey promise not to tell the other parent.

"Frozen lasagna again tonight," her dad would say, "I can't enjoy that unless I'm high." He'd slap the twenty in Joey's hand and then say, "Shh... don't tell mom." He'd wink and smile and leave.

Her folks were watching Jeopardy! when she and Cheese burst through the front door.

"Mrs. Wilkerson, I'm starving," Cheese said. "McDonalds was shut down, some lady had no head, and I couldn't get any french fries. What the hell is going on?"

"There's plenty of Pop-Tarts in the pantry," she said without looking.

They went to the backyard, each with their own pair of Pop-Tarts and some parmesan Goldfish.

"A sight like that calls for a fucking blunt," Joey said.

"Amen." Cheese could barely keep his food in his mouth he was chomping so hard.

"What do you think happened?"

"What do you mean?"

"To the lady, the lady with no head!" Joey unwrapped a Swisher and brushed the tobacco to the floor. She started picking apart a nug and filling the now empty cigar wrap.

"Oh, yeah, shit. You hear of spontaneous combustion? That shit's pretty real. I was reading about it the other day on the internet." Cheese shook his head. "I'm losing my high, though. I can't talk about important shit without a little THC in my head."

"You ever going to smoke me out?" Joey licked the paper and rolled the blunt tight.

"I provide comic relief. I'm the muscle. I'm the funny muscle."

"Doesn't mean you always get to smoke for free."

"You wouldn't cut me off."

Joey smiled and lit the blunt.

"Probably not," she said.

***

Infomercials on the Asian channel lulled Joey to sleep. Sometimes being stoned wasn't enough to pass out for her. It was hard to believe party-line services still existed but they did. Counting the number of ladies biting their lips was like counting sheep for her. After what felt like five minutes of shut-eye, Joey heard footsteps in the side yard. The footsteps got closer and the silhouette of a man passed by her window.

Her stomach turned.

"Holy shit."

She jumped out of bed, her whole body tingled with fear as she threw on some clothes and ran to her parents' room, just like she did when she was afraid of monsters under her bed at night. Her folks were snoring. She backed out of the room, deciding that it was best to leave them alone, hide under her blankets, and hope that whatever she saw was her imagination.

When she got back into her room, the shadow of a head was looking through her closed blinds.

"Fuck," she thought and stumbled around her room for her cell phone.

She dialed 9-1-1.

"La Palma Police Department," the dispatcher said on the other end. "How can we be of assistance?"

"There's a man in my backyard peering through my window."

"Honey, please don't call 9-1-1 for non-emergencies. I'll send out patrol as soon as they're available."

"How is this a non-emergency? If I'm dead tomorrow morning, is that the emergency?"

"It'll be an unfortunate circumstance of our budgetary crisis," the lady, disinterested, said.

"Fuck you!"

"Patrol's coming."

Joey hung up.

The figure tapped on the window. Joey froze and stared at its shadow. It walked away. She grabbed all the blankets on her bed and covered herself in them. She sat in the corner, her eyes fixed on the window. The police never showed up.

***

"That's some serious shit," Cheese said. "Some fucking guy was in your backyard last night, you called the cops, and nothing happened?"

"That's pretty much it," Joey said.

"Damn," Cheese shook his head and squirted ketchup on his hash browns. They were at Johnny's, a greasy spoon whose food was cheap enough to afford and tasted good enough to eat without regret.

"Have you seen Rock Lobster lately?" Joey asked.

"That dude fell off the face of the earth."

"Used to be an every other day customer. Haven't heard from him in a week."

Cheese cut up his over medium egg with his fork and stuffed it in his mouth. The yolk ran from his lips to his chin. It dripped a few times on the table before he noticed, wiped it up with his hands, and licked his fingers.

"Last I heard was he got fired from Subway for stealing cash out the register," Cheese said.

"Yeah, but I've seen him since then."

"He was breaking into cars, stealing shit, and selling it at pawn shops down in Hawaiian Gardens."

Joey poured some salt onto her scrambled eggs.

"He never told me that."

Cheese shrugged.

"He was probably embarrassed to tell you that he was buying weed with other people's iPods and shit. He's got some pride." Cheese shook the ice in his cup. "I need a freefill. You need anything?"

Joey shook her head. She moved her pile of eggs from one side of the plate to the other. Cheese stood up and headed for the soda fountain. Cheese came back with more Pepsi.

"You didn't even touch your food," he said. "Watch my shit, I gotta poop."

As soon as he left again, Joey's bandaged neighbor walked in by himself. He picked up a paper, ordered coffee, and took a seat facing her. He was wearing sunglasses and a cap, his bandages were crusty with blood, and no matter how hard he tried to look like he was reading the paper, Joey could tell his eyes were fixed dead ahead at her.

She shifted in her seat. She tried to stare at her eggs that were getting cold. She didn't know how to pretend to not notice.

Cheese came back to the table.

"Sometimes I can't relieve myself in a public toilet," he said. "I don't know how I feel about clean restrooms. If a worker is cleaning them up but doesn't wash their hands properly, that means they're cooking dirty food. I'd rather have a dirty toilet than shit eggs, know what I mean?"

"Shut up," Joey said. "My fucking neighbor just came in and he's been staring at me."

"You get so fucking paranoid when you're high, yo." Cheese picked up his last piece of bacon and examined it. "This shit is almost translucent. I specifically asked for extra crispy. I don't mind it being a little burnt. I hate when the fat is chewy."

A couple of police officers walked in. Joey slumped down in her chair and watched them. They ordered coffees and sat with her neighbor.

"I think I'm 'bout to go order some more bacon. See if they'll give me a deal, you know? Shit ain't right."

"Shut up. Shut up. Shut up." Joey pointed behind Cheese. "Don't look, though. What the fuck are the cops doing with that freak?"

"You're fucking paranoid." Cheese got up and went to the cash register.

Joey stared at her eggs but tried as best as she could to hear what they were talking about.

"...Drug dealer..."

"...Cleaning up the streets..."

"It's all too messy."

"What the hell are we doing here?"

"...Cliff's..."

That was pretty much all she could make of any of it. They all stood up at the same time and pushed in their chairs at the same time. Her neighbor didn't get up, he stared straight ahead at Joey.

Cheese came back with a plate of crispy bacon.

"They gave me extra for the fuck up. I told them I was their best customer and they shouldn't treat people like shit. They agreed. I also got them to change the channel. Nobody wants the fucking news this early."

Joey stared past Cheese at her neighbor. He finally stood up and pushed in his chair.

He walked past them muttering, "Mary, Mary, Mary, Mary, Mary," over and over again. He didn't acknowledge them, he looked straight ahead to where he was going, distracted by nothing.

"Your neighbor is a fucking trip," Cheese said.

"I think it was him in my backyard last night."

"He's harmless. Look at his fucking head, all bloody and shit. No worries."

Joey watched him as he left.

"You didn't even touch your food, man. I was gonna ask if you wanted any bacon but your plate is fucking full." Cheese leaned in over his pile of warm bacon. "Think of all the starving kids in Korea. What would they say about this?"

Joey stood up.

"You can have it. Hurry, though. I've got weed to sell."

Cheese piled his plate of bacon onto Joey's plate and started shoveling the food into his mouth.

"I'll meet you outside," he said and put up two fingers. "Two minutes."

***

"Sixty bucks," Joey said. Pete, a freshman at UCI, stumbled backwards a bit.

"Sixty bucks?" he asked and tried to get into Joey's face. Cheese pushed him away. "Last week it was fifty, this week it's sixty?"

Cheese chuckled.

"You're a smart kid, in college and shit, at fucking UCI studying biology. Don't they teach you nothing about supply and demand?"

"This is bullshit!"

"Yeah, well, start selling your own weed then if you don't like the prices." Joey put the bag back in her pocket.

Pete looked down at the pavement.

"Yeah, fine. Just sticker shock is all." He grabbed three twenties out of his pocket and gave it to Joey. Joey handed him the bag of weed.

"When you start sending your friends my way, maybe I'll give you some kind of friendly discount. An eighth a week doesn't cut it for discounts, though," Joey said as she and Cheese turned for her car.

"Is this what art historians do with their degree? Small time weed dealers?" Pete asked, thinking once they got to their car he'd be safe from their willingness to deal with him.

Cheese turned around and gave him a death stare.

"At least art historians know some basic economics, you punk bitch!"

Pete turned around and ran away.

Cheese got into the car and put on his seatbelt.

"When you going to get that fucking trunk fixed? It's been at least a year since that dumb ass hit you from behind. You're telling me you haven't saved a grand yet?"

"Holy cow, listen to you. You sound like my mom."

"I told you, it doesn't matter how small the accident is, you get the fucking insurance information. Your car is starting to smell like wet dog, anyways."

Joey turned on the radio.

"Don't try to ignore me. I bet a cat or an opossum climbed, somehow, into your trunk, gave birth and they all suffocated. It's starting to smell that bad, man."

"Shut up," Joey said. "It's easy to complain when you don't have a fucking car."

"I'm driving around with you scaring all the little Asian kids who give you lip."

Joey laughed.

"And for that, sir, I thank you. Roll up a joint."

Cheese started breaking apart nugs and spreading them evenly onto the rolling paper.

"It's a celebratory joint," Joey said.

"Oh, yeah? What for?"

"We're going to the body shop. Getting this fucking trunk fixed. On account of Pete's extra ten dollars, I have enough."

Cheese nodded. He lit the joint and drew deeply.

"Fuck yeah," he said, smoke accenting each word. "Fuck yeah."

"Get out your iPod. I think we need to hear some Tupac."

Cheese nodded.

"Fuck yeah," he said, "fuck yeah."

***

"Hey, yo, how long this is gonna take? I'm starving."

Joey just finished signing her name on the work order. She turned toward Cheese and shrugged.

"You know how it is, sometimes they say an hour and it takes thirty minutes. Sometimes they say thirty minutes and you gotta pick up your car the next day."

"You mean we could be stuck here all day?"

Joey nodded, sat down in the faux-leather waiting room chair and slouched.

"They never have any good magazines. Why the hell would I need to read Gun & Hunter in an auto shop?"

Cheese sat next to her and stared at the TV.

"I wish I learned how to read the bus schedule," he said.

"You've been carless all these years and haven't even learned to use the bus?"

"It's confusing, man. You ever tried?"

Joey shook her head.

"Never needed to," she said. "Always had a car."

"Me neither. You've always had a car."

Cheese picked up the OC Register and stared at the headline. He squinted his eyes and turned the paper around.

"Yo, I think I'm getting secret messages," he said.

"They say marijuana is linked to schizophrenia. You should get that checked out," Joey, eyes closed and hands folded on her lap, said, slumped in the chair.

"I'm just fucking around, but look at this." Cheese shoved the paper in front of Joey's face.

"I'm trying to sleep," she said.

"Orange County penitentiary says they're missing lethal injection serum," he said.

"And?"

"It's interesting, isn't it?"

"God dammit," Joey said, "just let me sleep."

Cheese threw the paper on the coffee table and stood up.

"Fine. Need anything from 7·11?"

Joey didn't answer.

"Fuckin' bitch," Cheese said under his breath as he walked out of the waiting room and toward the 7·11 across the street.

Joey kept her eyes closed and smiled as she tried her best to fall asleep but with FOX News on the TV, the constant coming and going of customers, and the guy who kept clearing his throat, she knew it was impossible. She got up.

"You guys have any coffee here?"

"What?" the older lady at the service desk with round glasses that covered most of her face asked. "For free?"

She smiled and rolled her eyes with a tiny grunt-laugh.

"Nothing's free, mama," she said to Joey. "You want coffee, you go to the vending machine and spend a dollar. It's a good deal, too. You also get a bigger Coke for a dollar but if you want coffee, you get coffee, yeah?"

"I suppose there's a drinking fountain or something, right?"

"Drinking fountain?" the lady grunt-laughed again. "Why we make a drinking fountain here? That's like sewer water. That's like pumped from the toilet after people flush. Come on. What we look like to you? You got a dollar you get a bottle water from the machines over there."

"The restroom's free, right?"

"What kind of asshole charges you to take a piss, huh?" the lady looked over her glasses. "Bathroom's always free, honey. Come on. What's with all the silly questions?"

Joey nodded and walked toward the restroom. It was unisex and had only one toilet which meant it was pissed all over. Good thing she didn't have any coffee.

She went to the sink and stared at herself in the mirror. There were bags under her eyes, her eyes were red, and she looked very stoned. She turned on the faucet and waited for it to get hot. She splashed some water in her face and then cupped her hands so she could get enough to quell her cottonmouth.

When she got back into the waiting room, the old lady at the service desk was on the phone speaking very quietly. When she looked at Joey, she averted her gaze as soon as Joey noticed.

Get me a coffee and some Hot Cheetos at 7-11, she texted Cheese.

She sat down and rested her head on the wall behind her chair. Five minutes passed before she felt a tap on her shoulder.

"Jesus Christ, how long does it take to go to 7-11?" she asked without opening her eyes.

"Ma'am, I need you to stand up and follow me," a brusque voice answered.

She got up.

"What seems to be the issue?" she asked with a faux legal authority.

"Just follow me. We don't want to cause a scene."

"I want your name and badge number before I do a god damn thing."

"What are you? Some fucking liberal?" He glared at Joey and pointed to the number on his badge, then he said, "My friends call me Bob O. You can call me that, too."

Seeing no way out of disobeying a cop's orders, Joey got up. He held the door open for her as she exited. Parked in the red zone was a white, windowless, van with no markings of any kind on it.

A man in a white lab coat came out the back.

"I want you to get inside the van," Bob O said.

"Tell me why first. I have rights, motherfucker."

"Everyone has rights, darling."

Bob O stuck two fingers in his mouth and whistled. Her car backed out of the garage, the trunk was open. It parked in front of the van.

"Take a look and you tell me why you're going for a ride with the law, sweetheart."

Bob O grinned. He was chewing on gum and yapping.

"Do you have to yap so damn much?" Joey asked.

"My nose is all plugged up, I have to chew with my mouth open. Deal with it." He put his hands on his hips and waited for Joey to take a peek at the trunk.

She walked slowly to the trunk and fixated her gaze at the dangling shoestring that hung just above the license plate.

"You know I haven't been able to get this damn thing open for months, right? That's why I'm here. I'm getting it fixed," she said. She had stopped advancing, afraid of what she might see.

Bob O nodded and kept chewing.

"Sure, toots. I know, I know. I hear it all the damn time. Just take a peek at those rights you care so much about."

She turned. Towards the open trunk. The shoestring dangled. She should have known what that meant a long time ago but she overlooked it. She should have known she never left a shoe, or a shoestring, in her trunk. All that she ever left in there were papers she didn't want to look at anymore. But as she inched closer, she knew something bigger was there.

Bloodied and lifeless, it was Rock Lobster's body. He had no head but she knew him by his shirt. He was the only person alive that still wore tie-dye t-shirts.

She stumbled backwards. Hand over her mouth. She heaved but nothing came out. She heaved again. They were all dry but nothing would come out. She felt tears but none came. She felt like screaming but there was no sound. She stumbled backwards, heaving and coughing, trying to yell but never quite getting it.

She backed into Bob O who grabbed her hands and put handcuffs on.

"You're under arrest. Anything you say or do doesn't really matter," he yapped in between chews. She didn't hear him.

Four men in white lab coats filed out of the back of the van.

Joey wriggled and screamed as each man claimed a limb. They carried her like a casket and, on the count of three, threw her onto an operating table. They taped down her head and she screamed.

"Time for the ball gag," one said and out of one of their pockets came a pink ball gag.

"Fasten it tightly," one said. "This one's a screamer."

"She seems crazy," the one at her right foot said. "Don't let her bite your fingers off."

"Who the fuck are you people?" Joey writhed but her head was strapped down so tight that any sudden movement made it feel like she was about to snap her neck.

All movement stopped in the back of the van. The men in lab coats let their hands fall to their waist. They shrugged in unison.

"Mary..." a voice from behind Joey grumbled over and over again. "Mary..."

Joey struggled on the operating table — she needed to get a look on that voice.

"What are you doing to my Mary?" the voice grumbled.

"Sir!" one of the lab coats said, "Sir, this person was found with a dead body in her trunk. We are simply following the proper procedures and codes you yourself wrote."

"This is my Mary! Get out of here!"

The lab coats looked at each other and waited for the other to be the first to obey. One finally did.

"We'll give him a few minutes," he said on his way out.

Joey squirmed to get a sight of the stranger. The stranger took the tape off her head. Joey's head turned instinctively to the stranger. He was silhouetted by the sun pouring into the Econoline but the smell of dried blood and the bandages curling off his face was unmistakable: it was her crazy neighbor.

He put his hand under her head as if to comfort her.

"Mary, you look so good since last I saw you," he said.

Joey spit in his face.

"Call me Gil again. For old time's sake," he said as he leaned over to give Joey a kiss.

Joey head bunted him and he stumbled backward, almost falling out of the back of the car.

"I know what it is, darling. It's my bandages. For old time's sake, let me take them off. We can be young again."

"Before you do that, Gil —"

"Ah, there it is. The sweetness of your voice calling my name in the morning."

"Before you take off your bandages, Gil, how about untying me from this fucking bed. What were you thinking?"

"My dear," Gil said, "My darling dear, I let my anger get the best of me. I should have never made our cars into moving death traps. I should have done what every other old man does and started a neighborhood watch."

Gil's hands trembled as he unfastened each strap. First her right foot, then her right hand. He knelt over for a kiss as he unfastened the left hand and then the left foot. As soon as it was free, Joey kicked Gil in the face. He stumbled backwards and tripped on his own foot as he fell to the ground.

"Mary, is this about the pickles?" he asked as he got himself back up. "I don't give a damn about the pickles. You make your sandwiches the way you want to make them. If it wasn't for you, I'd never eat."

His trembling hands went to his face and started to unravel the bandages.

"Mary, would you mind wrapping a fresh bandage around my face? This one hasn't been changed since you... since you... since you —" Gil fell to the ground sobbing, still unwrapping his face.

Joey stood up.

"I don't know who the fuck you are or who the fuck you think I am but I'm outta here."

"Since you died."

Gil got up. He grabbed Joey by the elbow and forced her to turn around. His skin was hanging onto his face only by brown and yellowed scabs. She could see his teeth through his cheek, his eyes had no eyelids, and his face looked like it had been boiled.

"You're not Mary," he grunted, "You're a fake! You're a fucking roach! You wouldn't be back here if you didn't kill her! You killed Mary!"

Gil put his hands around Joey's neck and stared into her open eyes as he watched her lose her breath.

"Hey, yo! Fuck Mary!" Cheese threw coffee onto Gil's face. Gil dropped Joey and screamed. Four lab coats wrestled Cheese down to the ground from outside. "Hey, Joey!" he yelled from the bottom of the dog pile, "I'll get you another coffee, no worries. He needed it more, though, you know?"

Gil's skin flapped off his face. Fresh blood pumped out and onto the interior of the van. Joey gave him a good punch and jumped out of the van. She slammed the doors behind her.

"Stop her!"

Baseball bat, baseball bat, there's always a baseball bat

She repeated this mantra as she ran toward the garage and jumped into the backseat of her car, where there always was a baseball bat. She grabbed it.

Clutch lock, clutch lock, you've always got a clutch lock

She reached into the passenger side floor and grabbed her trusty red clutch lock. She never used it for its stated purpose but it was Cheese's favorite threatening weapon when Biology majors at UCI gave too much lip about pricing.

Both weapons in her hands, she walked slow but confident back to the dog pile of lab coats on top of Cheese. Her mind was blank. Later, she would remember this moment as being in a trance but right now there was no word for it. It just was.

She could tell Cheese was putting up some kind of fight from the bottom of the pile by the amount of struggle in the lab coats' faces.

No matter.

He needed help.

She lifted the clutch lock above her head and slammed it down on the back of one of the lab coats' head. The other three jumped off of Cheese immediately. Cheese was bleeding, his nose probably broken, but he smiled as soon as he caught a glimpse of the red glory that was his favorite weapon. She tossed it to him.

"It's funny," he said as he swung from the ground on his back at the lab coats' ankles, "how getting punched in the face kills your high like that." Somehow, he found the time to snap his fingers. The lab coat whose ankles he was swinging at fell to the cement. Joey bashed his head in.

There were two left. They took one look at the fiery possession inside Joey's eyes, looked at each other, and ran away.

Bob O came out of the waiting room chewing a donut. He dropped it as soon as he saw the bloodied and beaten Cheese struggling to get off the ground.

"Fuck," he said and drew his gun. He pointed it at Cheese.

Cheese put his hands up.

Joey stared at the van, knowing that Gil was in there hiding.

She dropped her baseball bat and ran towards the driver's side.

"Halt!" Bob O shot a warning shot at the van. "Halt, god dammit!"

Joey got inside and started the car.

"You killed Mary!"

She could hear Gil screaming from the back. She was safe, though. There was a wire barrier between them and, although she could feel as his fingers poked through the wire to try and take her neck, she knew he was too weak to get any further.

She put the car in reverse and looked at her rear view mirror as Bob O fired over and over again into the car, missing her and Gil the entire time. He was too big to jump out of the way and just a second after the last moment she saw his screaming face in mirror, she felt the car go over him like a speed bump.

There was a cold prick in her neck and she felt a warm tingling throughout her body.

"This one makes you numb."

Her hands felt like they weighed a thousand pounds and she tried as hard as she could to open the door. There was no strength for it. She banged her head against the window.

Cheese came running up on the passenger side.

"Damn, you are one cold bitch," he said as he opened the door. "Your face is all droopy, what happened?"

"You killed Mary."

Cheese turned to see the barely fleshed face of Gil smearing blood all over the wire barrier.

"Oh, shit!"

Cheese jumped out of the car and opened the driver's side door. Joey slumped out. Cheese slung her arm over his shoulder.

"You gotta walk, J. You gotta walk. Help me out here, you're dead weighting."

As Cheese wobbled toward Joey's car and over the dead bodies they'd left behind, the back doors of the van flew open.

"Mary! You killed Mary!"

Gil ran out, a syringe in his hand, and lunged at Cheese.

Without thinking, Cheese dropped Joey to the floor.

"Ow!"

"Sorry, J. I owe you a Slurpee or something, shit!"

"This one paralyzes you!" Gil said as he grabbed Cheese's hoody and forced him forward.

Cheese socked him in the jaw, whatever remained of the skin on his face was pretty much gone. Gil fell to the floor, bleeding and screaming.

Cheese grabbed the clutch lock.

"No!" Joey yelled. "Wait!"

"What?"

Joey crawled, very slowly, to her baseball bat.

"I want to finish this fuck off."

"You need a Slurpee and a hot dog or something, yo. You don't have any strength."

But she lifted the baseball bat as far as it could go up, her arms, even to an observer, looked like jelly. The muscles had gone too relaxed.

It wasn't so much a swing as it was her body losing any strength to keep the bat in the air any longer. Her arms fell with the bat as gravity did its trick. The bat hit Gil in the head, not too hard, but hard enough to be the final blow to a man who had already lost most of his face.

Joey's body slumped to the pavement.

"Pick me up, you fat fuck!"

Cheese laughed and picked her up.

"We need to go back in."

"Are you fucking crazy?" Cheese asked. "More cops are going to be here any minute. We need to get the fuck out of here."

"Take me back in," Joey said.

Cheese shrugged. He walked through the door into the waiting room with Joey in his arms.

Joey slammed her keys down on the waiting room table. The lady stared into Cheese's eyes.

"Fix my fucking trunk," Joey said.

ACKNOWLEDGEMENTS

La Palma: A tiny town with two 7-11s, a police force armed with assault rifles, and a dive called Cliff's Hideaway. It is the town that I grew up in and it inspired *Death Thing.*

ABOUT THE AUTHOR

Andrew Hilbert lives in Austin, TX. He is the author of the chapbook of short stories, *Toilet Stories From Outer Space*, and a co-founder of the Weekly Weird Monthly. His poems and stories have been published worldwide, online and in print, since 2009.

You can keep up with all he's up to at his website: www.hilbertheckler.com.

Follow him on twitter @AHILBERT3000.